LITTLE WATERFALL

Harrison Abbott

ALSO BY HARRISON ABBOTT

NOVELS

Amazed Gloom

Filippo's Game

Polly's Dreams

Magpie Glen

Fox and the Birch Trees

Tannahills

A Trade of Grace

Down in Boxbush

SHORT STORIES

One Hundred Ticks

A SMALL NOTE

I'd like to dedicate this novel to my Uncle Basil, who, above all people, has always been encouraging about my writing.

Obviously this book is about an uncle as well ... The (main character) uncle in this novel is nothing like the real-life Basil Abbott. Ha. But I wanted to say thanks to the latter person in the only way I know how. Through written word. Cheers, Bas. x

PART ONE

1

It was the smell of cut grass.

We all know that strong smell, don't we? I remember this one summer in particular, when I was wee. It was super hot most of the days. And school was finishing up and the holidays were nearing. I was lucky enough to live next to the park. This amazing span of green that I could see from my window; and on every penultimate Sunday of the month, the lawnmower chap would come and reap up the grass.

He'd come in the tiny hours of the morning because the park would be busy by noon. And he couldn't do it in the weekdays because it'd be teeming with schoolkids – the school being at the tip of the hill above the park. Each third Sunday of the month he'd come and shred the grass and it brought this most enticing smell to me. He'd start at 5 a.m. And it was light even by that time – with that whirly magical sheen of dawn. I'd watch and smell and listen. Nobody else in the park but the mower. He did a pretty good job. Was usually done in ninety minutes. And then he'd drive his tractor/mower machine (whatever one calls them) away and the park was left vacant for me alone.

I'd sneak out of the house with my strip and boots and ball. And create my own world. I think I must've been seven years old. Played about with the ball, with these huge goalposts with no netting. Their rusty poles. And the pitch itself was embarrassingly uneven and lumpy. But I didn't think that way when I was a kid. The wet grass stuck to my studs and the skin of my legs under my shorts.

I can't recall where exactly the idea came from. But I'd imagine this person who was my teammate.

This guy called Johnny. Johnny was a man who was on the same team and we were both famous and playing in a raucous stadium. He'd be on the wing. And I'd do this fantasy over and over to myself, with John: I'd call out to him. He was belting down the wing and I was nearing the box, and I'd cry,

"Johnny: I'm here for you!"

And he'd pass it to me and I'd whack it in. Score. The crowds in the stands erupting.

And so I didn't even get somebody to physically pass to me in real life. I'd just station the ball outside one of the goals and then look over into the summery morning nothingness and yell out "Johnny I'm here for you, here to help!" and then I would take a pop at the empty posts.

I would have to sneak back home before my mother woke up because she would think me crazy for going out so early in the morning by myself. And take my boots off before I got in and be careful not to get any of the mushy grass on the carpet, in case she found out.

When I smell cut grass these days, as a man, it brings back all that boyish naivety. Makes me a stupid, middle aged man. Or rather, it simply makes me real. It's not a nasty scent by any means. And it is astonishing how memory can meddle with you like that, how it gives you cues via sentience. It's the same with when you hear a song which reminds you of a particular time, a film you went to see with somebody … the whole chronicle comes back to your mind in fragments. It's just not there in the present, anymore. It's lost, in time. And with most of these periods, it's only interesting to you. Nobody else cares. And mostly, you're able to dismiss it and think about something else.

But, with me, a freshly mown park in summer is unbearable and I cannot stand it and it sends me into memorial reels for days. And then I wish I never had that sanguine childhood summer. That it had never happened.

Just as I hate that my brother and his wife died, and that my nephew survived the accident. A lot of the resentment comes in knowing that my brother didn't even like me so much when he was alive. And I know for sure that his wife didn't. I was just a downcast nobody. And the only reason my nephew was given to me was because I was the only living relative. I was so ill-equipped to deal with an orphan.

And so if it were possible to bounce back in time and have *me* die in a crash instead of them. Or, more easily, for my brother to not take this or that turn on that road and pause at a traffic light instead of fluming through it. It was all chance and bad luck and that's what I mean. If they were to still be with us. Not me. 'Us'. Even if they still disliked me and weren't so keen on seeing me at Christmas. That would be fine with me.

Because I still can't know whether I hurt my nephew or not. Probably, yes.

I've never spoken to anybody about this.

I think I failed my brother's son. What does this say about me – and why should I pity myself rather than try and atone for it? Throughout this story I shall have to confess a lot. And maybe the reader dislikes me already. I may as well tell it bluntly. Just the way it occurred.

The problem is that I have no idea how to make up for it all. And it's not as if I deserve any help in a search for atonement. This is my guilt and crime and I must live with those themes and have them attack my health every day.

A funk of cut grass hurts me? It *should* do. Fair penance. Let it sadden my blood. Poison my memory.

Anyway.

Let's start with that day I got the surreal phone call.

3

I had CDs in my car of favourite bands. And, like most people, I used music to elevate my mood. Cheer me up. So I put on my favourite band to try and do that. When I sang along to the words, it all sounded different. As if I was hearing it underwater, and I couldn't concentrate on it that well, and I wasn't sure whether I loved it as much.

The radio was another option so I switched to that and they played music I hadn't heard before. But then on the hour mark they gave the news bulletins and there was all of this garble about a dodgy politician and these gruesome stats from the war, which didn't help at all. So I cut it off. And then I just had the dampened sound of the motorway before me, rushing at fifty mph. That and my own mind. I really didn't know how to cope with it. Mostly I was stunned. Didn't know how to adjust. I just had to get to this hospital and that was it.

And then I got there. This gargantuan car park and it took me ages to find a place to settle.

This all happened in June. And it was a sunny day and the shine shone on the cars as I crossed the park to the huge doors of the complex. There was a long queue before the reception bit. And when it was my turn I spoke to this young lady.

"Hi there," I said, and I told her what had occurred. It was a bizarre thing to say these facts. She nodded, and fiddled about on her keypad.

"You're on the wrong side of the building. You need to go to Block B and ask for reception there. If you follow the blue line you should find it."

I followed her orders. And walked through the hospital. The corridors were sticky under my shoes … at one point I walked passed this closed door and somebody was screaming inside and I couldn't even tell if it was a man or woman making the shrieking noises. Then I got to the B area. The smells changed, into a plastic-like scent and it got airy too. Then found the new reception. Where I met a man this time.

He told me to go to this specific room, where I would meet a Dr Joseph.

So I went there and I knocked on the door and a voice called "Come in?" Inside was a tired man, maybe twenty years my senior, who looked disinterestedly at me until I told him the details. He got up.

"Nice to meet you, my friend," he said and there was a tough handshake. His accent was foreign. I hadn't noticed that on the call earlier. "Come inside and shut the door."

"Sure, Doc."

"I can't imagine how you're feeling," he said, as he sat in his chair again, with me the other side.

"It hasn't really kicked in yet, Doc. It's just so surprising." The chair I sat on had this static felt, or fabric or whatever, and it crackled against my clothes as I moved. "Can you please tell me what happened with the crash? I mean. How the hell did it happen?"

"Your family were coming back from the cinema. It was a late showing and thus late at night. Your brother was waiting at a crossroads and waiting for the green light. It came. He went through. And didn't notice a van hurtling from the other side – somebody who had gone through the red. Missed it, rather."

"Who was the person in the other van?"

"A man. We don't know about that yet so I cannot tell you. But the police are involved."

"Well. What happened to *him*?"

"He's injured. But he's stable."

"Good for him. It was his fault, then? That caused the crash?"

"I do not know all of the details, sir. The police will investigate it."

"So he's here in the hospital as well? This other man."

The Doc noticed that I was starting to fume and I had a blush on my face. So I retracted. Eased the emotional flair down. (Though I still fantasise, to this day, finding out where the van man was in that hospital and going and killing him. Going into his room and murdering him. Then I would've gone to jail. It probably would've been a simpler history than all of which I'm about to tell you.)

"I've already passed on your details to the police," Joseph said. "You can even speak to them right now, if you want."

"No ... it's. No. Thanks though."

"Would you like a cup of tea or glass of water or anything Mr Ballard?"

"I'm good."

Dr Joseph had nice healthy white hair. I noticed as I spoke to him.

"Where is Caspar, Doctor?" I said.

"He's very close. I'll take you to him."

I was led to this small ward which was intensely quiet. There were older people in the beds – almost all of them were elderly and then were all wired up to masks and monitors and whatnot. Nurses would mosey around in their nice uniforms. It was all hushed and not even the machines made vocals and I went through the entire ward until we got to the end …

Where we met this boy lying with his back to us on one of the beds. He was six years old. Wearing a sky-blue hoody, the sheets pulled up to his torso.

Suddenly a great feeling of dread came over me. Of shame and regret.

Doctor Joseph went up to him first. He went around the other side of the bed and knelt down beside him, crouched down and spoke into Caspar's face. From this angle it didn't even look like Caspar was sleeping or whether he was alive; his shoulder blades weren't moving. And his skull shook lightly when Joseph talked.

I could tell that, just by the way Joseph acted, he was good with kids and was a father and probably a grandfather too. Whereas I was never natural with kids and had never had any myself. Was never easy with anybody.

"So," I heard Joseph whisper to him, "I've brought your uncle here to come help you. Your uncle Ralph. He'll help you out from here. He is there."

Joseph pointed at me. Caspar looked up at me – his head shot up and he turned and saw me. And this phobic spasm stung him. He winced. His jaw trembled. And he dropped back down on the pillow. Pulled the sheets up over his head and held them there. The he started crying. Sobbing.

The new noises of anguish filled the ward and I was humiliated that I'd caused them.

Joseph took me aside shortly after this; we went away

from Caspar's bed. He relayed the legal stuff to me in basic form. Because I was Caspar's only relative, I would be in charge of him temporarily. Yes, I got that.

"He hasn't slept in about thirty hours," Joseph said.

"Caspar didn't sleep at all during the night?"

"No."

"So he's ready for discharge physically?"

"He is."

"I'll take him home."

"Good."

"So when will the police get in touch with me?"

"I'm not sure exactly when but it will definitely happen."

"K. Hey – Doc? You know if there's a vending machine anywhere near here?"

"Huh?"

"You know, like for crisps and juice and stuff."

"Yeah there's one down the hall, through those doors. You need to go down the stairs though and so it's on the lower floor."

"Ta. I'll be back in five minutes."

I went out of the ward into this new area which was totally deserted and I found the staircase he was on about and as I went down them I had this image of throwing myself down them and breaking my body … but I didn't dare it, and I got to the bottom. This corridor was more public. Colours and people. I went downwards and found the vending machine. Checked my wallet and it was healthy and I bought a can of soda and packet of crisps and a chocolate bar. Then went back upstairs with the items.

When I returned to the ward Dr Joseph wasn't there. I came up to Caspar's bed, expecting Joseph to still be present but he wasn't. And so I had to approach my nephew myself.

He was lying the other side now. And he'd taken the sheets off of his face. He'd pulled the skyblue hood up instead and I could see the white triangle of his cheekbones and mouth.

I went around the side of his bed. To his side I mean ... and I didn't know how to engage with him, and hovered there for some time and didn't know whether he knew that I was there watching him. Eventually I decided to tap him on the shoulder. Softly. With my forefinger.

Caspar flinched. I did too. And nearly dropped the can of juice I'd bought for him.

"Sorry, Caspar," I said. And I bent down to him, trying to copy the way that Joseph had done it. But I failed in the mimicry.

He saw it was me. Froze. Then he closed his eyes. I worried that he might whimper again but he didn't. I held out the snacks to him.

"You want something to eat or drink, lil guy?" and I shook the crackly wrappers. Caspar opened his eyelids. He had these huge pupils. "Want some of the crisps? If you don't like the flavour I can get you another packet."

He looked at the packet I already had for him and he nodded and sat up. I opened the pack. And this smell of calorie chemicals and starch arose in the sterile arena. Caspar took the packet off of me. He started munching the chips. And the noise of somebody else eating is usually annoying but the fact that I'd fed him was now glorious. When he'd done with that I gave him the can of juice. I thought that I should've gotten him a bottle of water too so he wouldn't be dehydrated. After he drank I offered him the chocolate and he shook his head.

"The doctor told me that you haven't slept in a long long time, Caspar, is that so?"

He nodded.

"So why don't I take you back to my home. I've a spare room and I can make it cosy. We all need to rest. I can make you some Ovaltine. That always used to help me when I needed to sleep as a boy. Or I can buy you anything you like."

I was totally improvising here and it was lame and I could see that Caspar thought I was unimpressive as well. He blinked. The pupils were emotionless. This child didn't know me.

"Either way, lad," I said, "I have to get you back to a bed so we can get some shut-eye. Come on, my nephew."

I made to touch him again and he veered away from my palm. But he got out of the bed. His shoes were by the bedside table and he put those on. Then he stretched and yawned. Then I was tasked with leading him out of the hospital.

On the journey back to my city my nephew was in the back seat and I realised I had no clue how to speak to a child and it said a whole lot about my Asperger's and it brought up serious questions about what I'd ever been able to achieve anything meaningful in my life as a forty-something man and so as we were zooming down the motorway I turned to music again for help. Put on that beloved band. Set the volume at mellow. Caspar kept crying in the back seat. I could see him in the mirror. The tears trickled and trickled. All I thought I could do was keep the music on. Try not to crash *this* car. Mid afternoon now and the summery sheen dazzled the road and we could've been going on a holiday, my nephew and I. If I'd ever made an effort to get to know this kid, I thought, it wouldn't be so weird to be taking him some place with just the two of us. Moreover, all of these practical challenges arose to me as firsts; What would I do about the funeral for Tom and Miranda? Did Tom even have a will? How did the legal aggression work against this man that'd killed them? Was he drink-driving?

All of these things kept pounding me about the mind that day. And the clouds were especially brilliant. What are the names of the clouds – you know what I mean, how there are different styles of them? Those puffy titanic ones in pure white. Armada-like. Glorious. Those ships kept lording the sky and I would look up at them. And I thought *I used to appreciate those clouds when I was a kid. When I was Caspar's age.*

4

Caspar looked like my brother. They had the same eyelashes. Long and brown.

Yeah, Tom had been a good looking guy. I never was. And I was always a bit envious of that, jealous too. Because of pretty Miranda also. And I realised how silly it was, now, to have been threatened over something as trivial as being handsome.

I mentioned earlier that Tom used to invite me over for Christmas time. He did that out of a kind of duty, I believe, and I think he was a bit embarrassed of me as a sibling. Was being begrudgingly kind. If that makes sense? I mentioned to the Doctor Joseph (earlier on the phone) that I hadn't seen Tom in about two years. It was longer than that, in fact. Two and a half years, cos it was summer now and the last time I met up with his family was the Christmas before last.

It'd actually been the 27th December, I recall. Cos it was the day after Boxing Day. I'd gotten the train up there to his place. He lived in a lofty house in the suburbs and Miranda's siblings and their partners were around too. The in-laws had brought their children. A big lunch in the day time.

There'd been a storm that winter. The snow had disrupted the railway lines – and my train was delayed. So I turned up late. And missed the big lunch. Miranda was angry about that, but not to my face. I got to the house. Rang the bell and Tom greeted me in the doorway and he led me in to a living room filled with Miranda, Caspar and about eight other people of Miranda's extended family. I smiled and waved at them. Not one of them got up to come and hug me. (One of the in-law girlfriends shut her eyes down when she saw it was me. As if my mere image was visually unappealing. Though I can't even remember her name these days.)

Tom told Miranda I was autistic quite some time ago and I don't think she ever understood what autism is and I reckon she told the whole in-law clan too and, in turn, they had no understanding of it either.

Anyway. I sat with them in the living room around the live fire. Laughed along with them when somebody made a joke. The kids didn't go near me; Caspar included. I hadn't eaten that morning because I was nervous about coming at all. And I missed out on the lunch and then there was the lull between dinner. But they were all drinking in that sitting room minus the kiddies and I was offered some beers and tackled into them. It made things easier. Thus I drank on a lightweight stomach.

By the evening I was a bit hammered. Tom had said I could stay the night and he'd given me one of his bedrooms. Most of the guests had left already or were leaving. Caspar was put to bed (him being only four at that time). I thought I'd done fairly well – socially – for once in my life.

"Tom, buddy," I said to him when it was dark, "I think I might go a walk around the neighbourhood. I just feel like a jaunt. You wanna come as well?"

"Nah, bro, I'm quite tired. But go a walk by all means and I'll see you when you get back."

"Sound."

The storm had been and gone in his city and there were still scatterings of snow which flickered in rainbow dots under the starry sky. I smoked and I'd brought a beer with me and I made these clunky footprints in the whiteness, enjoying the crumply cushiony way it sounded under the boots.

When I returned to the house I let myself in quietly through the front door. Because I knew Caspar was sleeping upstairs. So I got inside and shut the door again tentatively. And was about to scuff my boots on the carpet ... when I overheard Tom and Miranda speaking in the living room, which was the first doorway in the corridor.

They were speaking about me. I knew because I heard them both using my name. I paused and listened.

"You say this every year, Tom," Miranda was saying, "and you never do it."

"I don't see what the dangerous problem is."

"It's not a problem. That's not what I mean – you *know* what I'm saying – it's embarrassing to have Ralph here."

"I don't find him embarrassing. He's odd ..."

"Ha! Yes, just a wee bit."

"But he's not aggressive or mean."

"Tom. Your brother drinks like a paratrooper."

"We've all been drinking heavily all night, Miranda."

"Yeah but we don't turn into a zombie like he does."

"This is my point: he does drink too, but he doesn't get angry or rude."

"Then how come the kids are all afraid of him?"

"He's an intense guy. Awkward."

"Is this the shit about the ADHD again?"

"Asperger's."

"Whatever. I never bought all of that baloney. Shrug. He should get some pills for it instead of getting drunk in front of the children."

"You do that as well, Miranda."

"I don't ..."

" . . ."

"Tom. Please don't invite him back for Christmas next year. Keep in touch with him, for sure. But I don't like him around my family."

And Tom didn't say anything. I wanted him to. He didn't.

And just then, Miranda started speaking again. I couldn't stand to hear more of her poisonous tongue. So what I did was, open the front door, noisily this time, and then shut it loudly: to make it seem like I'd just come in.

When I did this Miranda shut up instantly.

I had to act like I wasn't as hurt as I was. But I did it quite well. I got the snow off the boots and took my coat off and Tom came out of the living room and greeted me.

"Ralphie, my friend! How was your walk? Where about did you go – you were quite a long time."

"It was beautiful, Thomas, thanks. I'm quite sleepy myself now. Think I might retire upstairs for some sleep. But thank you for your hospitality as always."

"No problem, bro."

He went in for a hug and I offered him a handshake instead.

Then I went into the living room. Miranda was reading a book now in one hand and holding a wine glass in the other; she looked up and dealt me this brash smile with a full upper bar of teeth.

"That's me off to bed, Miranda dear," I said. "Many respects for all your lovely food today. Cheers for having me."

"Any time, Ralph. You're always welcome here any time. Night night."

I went to my room. Slept. Got the early train home

in the morning.

5

"You want something to eat, Caspar?" I said to him when we got into my flat.

He shook his head. He stood in the corner of the kitchen with his hands in the pockets of the skyblue hoody. I thought, shit, the boy didn't even have a spare pair of clothes with him. He had literally nothing. Except me.

For now I knew I had to get him to sleep. The longest I've ever been awake for was about twenty five hours when I was twenty something, travelling in Europe, when I still had the energy to do so.

Caspar looked dazed. As if he might collapse.

I heated up some milk for him. Ovaltine! Like I suggested earlier. And whilst the pan was boiling I sat him on the couch in the living room. (There were empty bottles and cans dotted around the place and I was ashamed. So I cleared those up and took them to the recycling.) And I went into my other bedroom.

I'd been afraid that the place would be a total tip. It wasn't. Rather a bit sterile and musky. There was a single bed in there. And my old bike which I hadn't used in months cos I'd been too lazy to fix the punctured tyre. So I wheeled my bike into my room and then I smelled the milk burning in the kitchen.

Yes, it'd burnt at the bottom of the pan. I was fucking-up already. I cleaned the pan up. Then did a new milk for Caspar and finished a mug of Ovaltine for him.

"Have you ever had this drink before?" I asked when I handed it to him.

He didn't respond. Only held it by the handle. And smelled it. I felt that he was intimidated, waiting for me to react. Which I was. So I went away to Caspar's new bedroom again and left him to it.

The sheets on the bed were all white and dusty. I took those off. In the corridor cupboard I had some others I picked the most colourful ones. And I opened the window too … and in my room I had this bedside lamp which gave off this apricot glow. So I put it in Caspar's room instead. What else could I do? I thought about leaving some painkillers by his table but then remembered six year olds can't take painkillers. About leaving some books for entertainment. But all I had in my flat was hardcore literature which he wouldn't be able to understand. (I did used to have a few of those *Beano* and *Dandy* Annuals ((remember those?)) recently. But I'd given those away to a charity shop just last year. Damn.)

What about kids' shows? Or a film. For him to watch?

So I went to my DVD collection and looked over the titles for something appropriate for him to see. And most of it was like my book catalogue: miserable and not-for-tots. But but but, there was one kids' flick which I'd bought out of nostalgia ages ago.

It was *Robin Hood* (1973). The cartoon version. I used to watch that endlessly. Thought he might like it. I went through to the kitchen with the DVD in hand.

Caspar hadn't touched his Ovaltine. I looked at it. He hadn't moved from his corner either.

"My man," I said to him, presenting the movie, "come and lie down in the other room. I'll stick this film on for you in the background."

He was so exhausted he couldn't register with my words. I ventured towards him to touch him, to guide him out of the room. He dodged my hands, and seemed to get what I was meaning, and followed my gesture out, and I led him into the new room and up to the bed. He got into the bed and I put the covers over him.

I didn't have any pyjamas for him either. I would go and buy him some in the morning. Or actually, go and do that tonight, since the supermarket was still open – they still sell clothes.

My laptop was in my room so I got that and brought a chair with it into Caspar's room. Hooked the computer up on the chair so he could see it from his pillow and I put *Robin Hood* in and looked at him.

"Can you see it okay from here?"

His eyes were almost glued up. I hoped this was a sign that he might just be headed off to slumber. So I lowered my voice.

"Caspar. I'm just through the hall in the kitchen. So if you need anything then please call out for me or come and get me. I'll be on point."

I put the volume on the laptop down to half-way.

Shut the curtains on the window. And let him sleep.

I considered kissing him goodnight but I am not the person who does that kind of thing as you have probably already guessed; my lips probably would've been acidic versus his young skin. Instead I left his door open just a little. And his body looked just like I'd seen it in the hospital ward earlier – his shoulders thin, spent, immobile.

6

Caspar didn't speak for four days. He barely made a sound. And it was an unprecedented thing to have this stranger in my flat who wasn't talking at all.

The morning after the *Robin Hood* night I went out and bought him some new clothes. Which was also super odd. Though it would've been worse if the child were a girl, as I know nothing about fashion or whatnot.

I booked some time off work and my boss was understanding. I just put through my holiday pay, which had been stacked up cos I'd never used it. So I didn't have to worry about that in the meantime.

At the same time, Miranda's sister Kelsie had been in touch with me over the phone. We were discussing what to do regarding the funeral. And discussing the Tom and Miranda's respective wills, now that they were dead.

Tom's lawyer had gotten in touch with me to transfer Tom's will over. He sent it via email.

And I was surprised by the contents.

The main part of interest to this story was that it said something along the lines of: 'If I die by accident and my wife passes too, I'd like guardianship of my son passed onto my brother Ralph'. Not in those words. But that was the order within his will.

(Tom had also left me a fair amount of money. Which I wasn't expecting either. His wealth and status were the other things I'd forever coveted. He was more successful than I was. For a whole host of reasons. And now that he had perished I again felt guilty for not having appreciated him as a family member. My only one. Our folks had both passed of cancer. Mother ten years ago, Dad fifteen.)

Kelsie was one of the members of that awkward festive bash I told you about earlier, when I arrived late; she was there in the living room. I'd only had about three small-talk conversations with her in my lifetime. In short – I didn't know well at all.

I agreed to call her the evening after Caspar had first arrived at my place. This occurred in the evening and Caspar was dozing in his room. I was a bit jittery about the call and so I took a few beers in beforehand. So I called her at nine o'clock which was the time she suggested.

"Hello?" she answered.

"Hi there, Kelsie. I'm so sorry about what happened to your sister."

"And you with your brother."

"It's a great tragedy. I hope you're coping well?"

"I'm grieving out of my mind."

"I am too," and this sounded like a lie and it definitely was. I was numb. Numb and nothing else. I hadn't chosen a correct emotion yet. And my voice sounded robotic. "So what did you want to chat about specifically this evening Kelsie?"

"Well, the funeral details. It will be in a week's time. And the ceremony will be for both of them of course, buried next to each other," and she went on with a full list of details. It seemed she had a pretty good grasp of the situation.

I told her I would contribute to it financially of course.

"Thank you for organising all of that then Kelsie. I'll bring Caspar up that day early."

"How is he?"

"Caspar … He's very quiet. But I've bought him

some new clothes. And he's eating fine. I'm showing him cartoons and films. Kids' movies, you know. He rests a lot."

"But how *is* he?"

"Very sad. He weeps a lot."

"I will come and see him."

"Okay."

"I know he'd like that. He and I were always close. Can you give me your address, Ralph?"

I told her it.

"I'm free on Tuesday daytime," Kelsie said. "I will drive over and see him at your place. That all good?"

"Sure. Sure. Umm. Would you like me to do anything in the meantime Kelsie?"

"I think we should just get through the funeral first. And then we can chat about the legal work in the future. Sound like a deal?"

"Okay, right."

"Speak to you on Tuesday then Ralph."

And so there were four days were Caspar was silent and on the fifth day Kelsie came. I'd told him she was coming. When I dealt the news he livened up a bit, and got out of the bed. He ate some cereal in the kitchen with me instead of his dark room. Then the front doorbell pinged. He ran to the door. I opened it to her. Kelsie was a pretty lady like her sister.

Caspar jumped into her and she crouched down and they hugged each other hard.

"I've missed you," was what Caspar said. All three words daggered me. They hurt. As I stupidly stood, watching them.

"And you, little Caspar," she said and kissed him

with her petal-like lips.

They clung together for quite some time and they whispered in each other's ears. When they'd finally unravelled Kelsie stood up and she smiled at me. There was an off key handshake. Which usually happens between men and women; where the male grasp is tough and the female grasp dainty and they don't work well together. But that's probably just me being me.

I invited them in.

I'd prepared some bakery stuff. Croissants and so on, and fancy coffee which I didn't normally drink and some pulpy orange juice, cos that's what I thought I was supposed to do. Kelsie accepted. So I put some croissants on to bake. I'd gotten some yoghurts and sesame snacks for Caspar.

Kelsie and Caspar sat chatting at the table whilst I prepared the food. I couldn't really hear what Caspar was saying, but he was smiling as well as crying a bit too – his face had colour again, pink and shining.

I brought the food over to them and joined them at the table. Caspar sat on her lap and his eyelashes when he looked up at her fondly were more spectacular than ever. (I didn't get why the coffee was this expensive; it wasn't even that tasty.) He gobbled his yoghurts down. And then Kelsie, looking out of the window, said,

"It's such a sunny day, Caspar, do you want to go out for a walk?"

"Yeah, please."

I got the correct feeling that I wasn't invited. Nor did I really want to go with them. Caspar put the skyblue hoody on and left the flat with her, holding her hand. And for half an hour I had the place to myself again. I cleaned the table up. And stuck the radio on and I sneaked a little whisky into me. A few shots before they would get back and there were all of these blunted emotions swirling in my mind and the whisky helped to ease them up. Or perhaps I hoped it would.

Being in the flat wasn't like what it used to be at all.

Then they came back home and the present fable continued. Caspar was flushed. Kelsie had gotten him some of those *Kinder Surprise* eggs with the toys inside of them. And this had overtaken his concentration at the table. I offered Kelsie another coffee and she said yes please. Whilst Caspar was enraptured Kelsie came over to me at the kettle and she spoke into my neck,

"Ralph. Can I speak to you in the other room just for two seconds."

"Of course."

I worried about what she was going to say and I couldn't guess what it was and I led her down the corridor into my small living room. Kelsie shut the door lightly behind us.

"Ralphie," she began, with a stern face, "I know this is horrible time for all of us. And you've just lost your brother."

"Right …"

"But you have to realise that Caspar is a great kid."

"He is."

"And he's probably got the hardest situation of all of us right now."

"He does."

"So you need to help him."

I didn't understand what she was saying.

"You have to try and communicate with him a bit

better," and when I blinked at her, she continued, "when we were out walking earlier, Caspar told me about you. He said that you barely ever speak to him. He doesn't know if you like him or not."

I blushed. I couldn't remember the last time I'd blushed, not for years. She saw the blush – and it made her entitled, more than she already was.

"Kelsie. This child has not spoken in four days. He's in grief. His parents got killed and he was there when that happened. There's no wonder he's a bit quiet."

"You're not trying to speak to him, Ralph, is what I think. I know that you have your *condition*, or whatever it is. But that's not an excuse."

"You have no clue what you're on about."

"Your condition."

"You do not have any frame of reference here, Kelsie. You dunno what you're talking about."

"There's no point in being rude to each other. I just wanted to suggest to you politely … or, tell you, that that's how he feels at the moment. You should *be more nice* to him."

"I will. He's still my nephew: why would I not do that?"

"Well, why aren't you?"

It was hard to express how furious I was because what she was saying was so astonishing. But I have always been half a coward. Anger seemed to belong in my younger days. In my teens and twenties when I was constantly getting into trouble, a lot of it due to my own ill temperament. In my latter years I learned to be meek. Even if I disliked that. To crumple in meekness was the easier option. That's what I did now.

"I hear what you're saying, Kelsie."

"I'm sorry Ralph. I didn't mean to hurt you I'm just fearful for Caspar is all."

"It's okay; no worries."

"OK. Well. I'm going to need to head back home this afternoon. But I'll see you in a few days at the funeral?"

"Definitely."

Kelsie turned and made to open the door to leave. She hesitated and turned back.

"Oh, Ralph there's one other thing I forgot to mention. About the funeral. Me and some others are going to say some words at the ceremony. I have something I'd like to say to the group about Miranda. Would you like to do that as well? You can say your bit. If you want?"

"Hmm. I hadn't thought about that …" at first this idea seemed awful and I wanted to say no right away. Public speaking was not a skill I owned. But I wanted to be polite. "Can I think about it Kelsie and then I'll get back to you?"

"That's fine."

Then she left and I stayed in the living room and she went to say bye to Caspar. He was sad that she was leaving and didn't want her to do that and he got teary all over again.

7

I was close to my father when he was still around. If you'd like to call me an Aspie then my Dad almost certainly was Asperger's as well. He was a gruff, practical man, who was quite keen with his hands when it came to discipline. I'm not calling him a tyrant; he was just old fashioned that way and knew how to skelp you if you got negligent. And he did that up until quite a hefty age. He was probably Alzheimer's for years before he finally went, and Mum was there to aid him rather than have him shipped off to a Home.

Dad fought in the war. The most famous one; the war they make films about ever since it stopped in the previous century. And I've always been pretty proud of that. (Cos he fought on the good-guy side; in the only ever moral war in history.) He was part of those theatrical days. I've still got his medals. Which he left them for me specifically.

Father bore me after he came home from Europe. I have vague memories of him from childhood. Most of which were out in the garden where I'd work with him on his crafts; he showed me how to use tools and was skilful and strong with them. I wanted to impress him by matching his abilities.

There was a spring morning I remember poignantly. I think it was Easter actually, because I was on a school holiday and was all gleeful with the freedom of it ... and was helping Dad in the shed. We were mending something. One of the chairs in the house which had a broken leg.

I can't recall the exact the details except that he was teaching me how to use a chisel. Because we needed to widen the hole to fit a new leg into it. So he showed me the basics of a chisel and how to chip away at the wood. And he told me *not* to do it this way, else I might get injured.

Dad asked me if I was able to work by myself whilst he went outside to smoke his pipe. (He was a voracious smoker and I still don't know how tobacco didn't eventually kill him; he chain-puffed his pipe daily and the house was filled with ashen trays and he always reeked of it himself.)

And I do not recollect exactly how the accident happened:

My finger suddenly bloomed with blood. I'd committed what he'd warned me not to do. I dropped the tool and was worried that he might've heard it – he was whistling in the garden. But then my finger just pumped and pumped and he was bound to notice the wound. Therefore I was stuck inside the hot shed with this silly tissue around my finger and it wouldn't stop bleeding and I was ashamed that I had failed at the job and that I hadn't followed his directions. And I knew if I went out and confessed to him that I'd cut the finger he would explode. I'd probably get a smack as well. And all the while he whistled that famous oldie folk song and the birds and grasshoppers sang in tandem with him.

Should I go out and confess or should I stay here and let him find me? I hovered there for minutes until he finished his pipe. And then I thought he was coming towards the shed because I heard his footsteps, so I gallantly went out to the garden to meet him. But, Dad was going into the house instead. And I stayed there on the sunny grass until he came out again.

He carried a mug of coffee with him and he drank it and paused and looked up at me and the steam's vapour caught in the sunray around his face.

"Dad," I said, "I made a mistake." And I took the tissue off the finger, hoping that the gore would lessen my verbal delivery.

He smiled.

"Ah, son," he said, "that looks sore."

"You're not mad?"

"Ho ho. Why would I be mad?"

"Because I used the chisel wrong."

"Ha. You think you're the only man to use a tool wrong for the first time? Don't be hard on yourself."

He came over to me and looked at the cut.

"That's quite a deep one though. Run inside, Ralph. Clean out the cut with water and hold it down with a cloth for a while. Then stick a plaster on it. Understand?"

I did as he said.

The finger didn't stop bleeding for some time. And I was too embarrassed to go back out to the shed to keep working with him that Easter.

I've thought about that memory a lot ever since and I've never been quite able to 'figure out' why it bothers me. If you get me?

There's a scar on my finger from the incident, worn and faded now; it's not the most impressive of scars but the mark is still there.

8

I didn't hear Caspar speak for the following three days either. He was distraught after Kelsie left and I couldn't do much in order to bond with him after that.

Before Kelsie said what she said I'd actually thought I'd been doing that. Bonding. After I heard what he'd said about me, I reacted regressively. Immaturely. I got offended, and self-pitied, that he didn't seem to like me and didn't appreciate all I'd done for him since the fatal incident. In the kitchen when he was sleeping I drank alcohol in secret and all of these hideous feelings went through my mind. *I wish he'd died in the crash as well – it would be so much simpler. Have a funeral for all three of them. Nobody in the family cares about me anyway. Why should I have to be the one who looks after this orphan?*

Why doesn't Kelsie just take him? Caspar obviously loves her and not me: so why can't she do the work? He's got Miranda's slime in his DNA. The same slime as Kelsie does. So why doesn't she adopt him? And good riddance to both of them!

There were numerous occasions when I thought about calling Kelsie and asking her if she and her husband could take Caspar off me. I didn't need the liability. Did not want to fuck a young mind up with me (a historical fuck-up) as a guardian. It would've been better to have her do it – raise this kid.

But I was stubborn as well.

Tom had legally dealt this child to me. And perhaps I could be a good uncle if I were to try harder. I'd only been trying for a few days anyway.

And so I did as Kelsie had suggested, those three days leading up to the funeral. I tried to get chatting to Caspar about stuff.

I brought out the retro videogame console with the classic games and had to hook it up to the old TV cos the modern one wasn't compatible, and tried to ignite his interest in that but it didn't work and he just wouldn't speak. I'd try questions over and over;

"Caspar, do you wanna go out to the cinema this evening?";

"Would you like to go down to the pizza restaurant at the end of the street – they do fab food?"

"Do you like swimming Caspar? I can drive you over to the big famous pool. We can go and get some trunks for you before that too?"

He literally didn't respond. Shook his tiny head and that was all and it made me the loser and the degenerate that I was.

Before the funeral I went down to the posh clothes store and bought him a little suit for the funeral. Black clothes and a white shirt. Shoes as well and then I dressed him up in the morning. It was tricky and intense and Caspar didn't really get what was happening. He did, in a way, but not really. Caspar didn't understand why he was being dressed up so smart – as if he were going to a celebratory event.

Then I put him in the car and took him to the next city to watch his parents get buried.

9

200 people turned up to the funeral. Maybe more. A lotta folk.

Many of them didn't know who I was until Kelsie introduced them to me: and their initial disinterest from my appearance changed into these heartfelt words, these frowning brows. I'd never even met 90% of them. Friends of friends, mostly from Miranda's side.

There was one man who was Tom's best mate and had been his best man at his wedding and I had met him several times ... and he didn't recognise me when I saw him. Dylan, was his name. He was the only person who I spontaneously ventured to greet.

"Hi there Dylan," I said, shaking his hand. He shook the hand and I could see him failing in semantic connection as he looked at me.

"Hey ..." he said.

"How are you doing?"

"I'm good. Well, I'm *not* good, of course! But, it's nice that so many people have turned up today. Umm, are you ... Remind me of your name, sir?"

"Ralph. Tom's brother."

"Oh, Jesus. I just didn't recognise you: you've changed so much since I last saw you. Ha ha ha."

And he wasn't even ditsy when he realised his glitch. He just grinned and went on to talk about something else as if nothing had happened.

Elsewhere, Kelsie took care of Caspar. Everybody was glorious around him and he absorbed all the attention.

I smelled alcohol off of a lot of people. And I

could tell many of them had snorted or taken pills or whatnot before they attended in order to get through the grief. But that was all garble – they were just taking the liberty to do that since they now had a day off work. Many of them were in their twenties and many were couples. That boyfriend/girlfriend shite, all-so-in-love now and most of them would be enemies in five years' time. I had no interest in them.

Ultimately, I was one of the very few blood relations of Tom's at the occasion.

The whole setting was a grand kirkyard – I shoulda said already – with a mighty church. Kelsie had paid for the Minister to lead the solemn send-off affairs, which were conducted inside the building as if it were mass or Sunday service. I found this ironic because I knew that Tom despised religious stuff and he was never into it. Once upon a time, he told me that Miranda considered herself Christian and so that was probably why. Meh, what did it matter now?

We sat inside the church. I sweated, as did a lot of people, it being a merry midsummer day and the sunshine beamed through the stained glass Saints and I watched the colours as the Minister spoke about my little brother who was now dead. He was a good talker, for sure. He'd never met Tom in his life. I wondered what it was like to be a Minister in the modern era – within a culture of mass atheism.

And then Kelsie got up to the podium and started talking about Miranda. Kelsie was an all right orator as well until she choked up and got blubbery and it turned diva-like and I wondered whether I was the only cynical bastard in the vicinity who found her gut- wrenching. Apparently so, cos when I looked around there were all these young ladies wiping their cheeks and men holding their faces down. When she finished there was an eruptive applause. A fine performance.

Dylan (Tom's best man) followed her. And his style was all jokey and laddish and he got out the chuckles from the mass in the arena. So he told several anecdotes about his drunken funnies with Tom ... and at points the whole population was laughing. I thought how absurd it was that alcohol could be used as a funny in one context and be totally abysmal and shaming in another. When he cracked the lines I smiled and smiled and I wanted to burst my tomato cheeks. Spike the blood out of them and watch the liquid flume.

And then Miranda's father was on next. He was this elderly chap and he was visibly shattered and he was the only person that brought out pity in me and made me realise how mean I was internally. His voice was quiet. He spoke about his daughter when she was a girl and his diction was muddled and shuddery but we appreciated what he was saying. He finished.

Right:

Remember Kelsie asked me to say some lines at the funeral?

I accepted her offer and said I would. And I didn't know it would be like all of this, in a grandiose church with this many people. And everybody else had done brilliantly. I did not wish to do it anymore. (I hadn't even written a speech on paper or anything; was expecting a jumble of informal sentences around a table, or something.)

Kelsie then announced to the congregation,

"And now Ralph, Tom's brother would like to say something."

It was impossible for me to say no now. So I was walking up to the podium with all of these eyes on me. Kelsie gave me this 'be brave' face which didn't work on me. The walk-up was tricky but when I was at the podium this blankness washed across me. When you're in front of a stadium of strangers you can be somebody else. Can improvise.

I swallowed. Breathed. Rubbed my grey hair.

"Tom was my younger brother," I began. "He always had that magnetic presence around people … which is why so many of you are here. He was clever and cunning and that's what made him wealthy and popular.

"At the same time. As I was listening to all of these words said recently. From the previous talkers. You were talking about Tom as if he was an angel. This blissful human being. All of you lauded him on how sublime he was.

"Dylan – yeah. Dylan, you went on and on, describing him as a 'pure brother' and so on. That he was the most stand up guy you ever knew.

"But you didn't know Tom when he was a kid, or a teen. You met him in your stupid university days. Nobody in this room knew Tom as well as I did when we were boys. And I can tell you that he was not an angel. Instead, he was the opposite of whatever that's supposed to mean:

"He was a mean, sadistic boy. And he stayed that way throughout his manhood. A naturally nasty guy. That's the reason why I shunned him across my life. He was not a good human in any generic sense. I don't see why I should pretend that he was. He was not a supervillain. Wasn't a moral person in an everyday way either.

"But. But … but. I'll miss him anyway. He's my

only sibling and I'd like it if he were still alive. Now that he's gone I wish that I hadn't been so cold. And I wish him glory wherever he is today.

"It's just that it's a travesty, hearing all this luscious acclaim about him being a great man when this wasn't quite the case. This doesn't mean that I didn't love him or hope that his soul is well now, whichever place it's at right now.

"Uhh. That's about it. Thank you."

I left the podium and went back to my seat and there was this profound hush in the audience for several seconds and then somebody started clapping and this infected others to do the same and they did it out of sheer bewilderment and I was glad that this was the case.

10

What about my mother?

She was a complacent, bubbly woman who everybody liked and she was chronically embarrassed of me. When we were out in public on the weekends there would be many a person who would stop and chat to her. She would keep me behind her legs. To hush me away. I didn't understand when I was that small.

The irony was that she drank a lot. Probably where I inherited it from ... the addictive behaviour with beer. But I can't be a sad bastard and blame my thing on somebody else.

I told you a memory about my father and so here's one about her.

She enjoyed cheap red wine and would get comatose from Thursday through to Sunday. One Thursday, I was rummaging about in her bedroom. I was looking for a new jotter to write a story and knew that she had lots of notebooks and artsy stuff in her belongings. A lot of which she never used.

So I figured I would go and pilfer one of them cos I had this new story keen in my head.

Amongst her collection I found this handsome blue hardback jotter and I wanted it.

Opened it up. And I discovered that she had written within the initial pages. The first two or three pages.

I really wanted the book for me and not for her. So I ripped out her handwritten pages and crushed them up and threw them in the bin ... and sneaked back to my room with my new jotter.

(What age was I? Probably seven or eight. This doesn't make it excusable.)

I thought I'd gotten away with it. Until I heard this shrieking from her room. A few hours later. And she came into my room. She was all crimson and leaky.

"Did you take my book Ralphie?" her voice was slushy. And then she saw the jotter. I timidly handed it to her.

There were a few lines of my story in the first pages.

She saw the marks in the spine where I'd torn out her pages.

Mother collapsed and started crying.

"Did you take out my journal pages?" she blubbered.

"No no no I didn't." And my eyes got shiny too because I was ashamed that I'd hurt her.

She hung against the radiator and sobbed and asked me over and over again. It was early evening. (She had this prominent belly and apple cheeks and she was never really centric within one mood or another. With mother, it was a colour wheel of characters – if you knew her intimately. She was bizarrely charming with people in public. Indoors, she could be one person one day and that person's arch enemy the next. She would change and change, change constantly – she shifted about without knowing it. It was maddening to be raised by her and I've not met a single person like her since.)

Dad had heard her wailing and he arrived on the scene. He glanced around the room and sussed what had happened. I feared that he might scold me for what I'd done. But he didn't shout at me. Mother was just rapt with agony on the floor. He picked her up and led her through to her room again. He turned the lights off and let her sleep. Then came back to me. He was strict and soft.

"Did you rip out the pages of her diary, Ralph?"

"Yes."

"Why?"

"I just wanted a new book to write in … It was silly. I'm sorry."

"You can't do that with other people's stuff Ralph."

"I know."

"Where are her pages then?"

"I mushed them up."

"*Why*?"

"I don't know."

"Right … Well. I want you to get the crushed papers, and the jotter, and put them in the street bin, okay? Not our one but the one at the end of the street. Because hopefully she'll forget about it. That you did this. I'm surprised with you, Ralph. You feel bad about what you've done?"

"Yeah."

"You should. Now, go and bin the jotter."

I did as he said.

Outside the street was silent and twilit and I wasn't usually allowed to go out by myself this young and it felt good but at the same time I didn't fathom what had happened tonight. I put the pretty blue jotter and the shredded papers in the street bin and nobody saw me do it.

My father had been correct. Mother never remembered about the jotter. And nobody ever got to know what were in her diary entries within those pages of which I'd robbed from her.

11

Barely anybody spoke to me for the rest of the funeral. Kelsie didn't speak to me nor did I try reach her. And there was one moment where I caught Dylan giving me this aggressive glare. I looked off. Was too old for antagonization.

My brother and his wife were lowered into the earth in these fancy coffins. I took my coat off; it really was pipingly warm. It was difficult to imagine Tom being in that wooden box, as handsome as it was. It was as if the coffins might've been filled with air and that there was no reason to put them underground. And when the sight of his coffin finally disappeared from land level – this enormous roughness clenched around my throat and my kneecaps shook. I watched him go. Even though it seemed his body wasn't there. I hoped it would be up in the sky or some other planet where he was relaxed and himself hoping that all of us weren't suffering so much.

When that part was done there was a plan for an afterparty. For the kids to go home and the adults to get drunk and eat cheese; Kelsie had booked out a restaurant. This seemed like an insane idea to me (to have a party for two people who have just perished) and I had already decided I wasn't going. Plus, I had to drive Caspar back home.

So when the burial shit was complete I sought my nephew out in the crowd. Everybody was milling out of the graveyard towards the cars at the back of the church.

I found him next to Kelsie's husband Mark. Mark grimaced when he saw me in a similar way to Dylan. Shrug, I couldn't care.

"Caspar," I said to him. "I'm heading back home. Are you wanting to come with me or stay here with Mark and Kelsie?"

He seemed confused. Not scared or conflicted, just a bit baffled. His face was all puffy ... but from tiredness as well as emotional heft.

"I'm just going to drive back to my place and I can make you something to eat and stick on a film, my lad," I said, "but if you'd rather go home with Kelsie and Mark then that's fine too."

He nodded.

So at first I thought he meant he wanted to stay with the in laws.

"Okay, well I can bring your stuff over to Kelsie's tomorrow then. That's fine."

Then he frowned and shook his head and came towards me.

"Oh," I said, "you mean you'd like to come back with me?"

He nodded and I was really surprised and touched.

"Come on then boyo, the car's this way."

I was gonna offer Mark a handshake but he was still staring at me in that macho way and so I just thought fuck it and turned from him and led Caspar off to the car. We got inside and I drove us out of the car park.

And that was Tom's funeral.

On the ride back I felt a righteous shame over what I'd done in the church. And I kept looking at Caspar to see whether he was angry. I wouldn't have said those things if it were just me and a six year old boy in a car, so why did I say them in front of two hundred people?

It had happened and was carved in history and I would have to deal with the judgement of it.

During the event I had decided that I would 'give Caspar up' to Kelsie and her family. And my question to him in the car park was my way of asking him what he felt about that. I was still stunned that he'd chosen to come back with me; but then again maybe he didn't know what I was meaning.

When we got back into my city my plan was to ask him a second time. Offer him, rather, the option of going to live with Kelsie and co. It would be better for him. She was a mother already and knew how to raise tots. I didn't. He'd survive with them.

But it would be mean to bring that up for a second time for today. I couldn't read him in the car because he showed no emotion and wasn't crying and he actually fell asleep in mini bouts. He was still sleeping when we showed up to the flat again. So I lifted him up and carried him upstairs. Caspar weighed as much as a dog would. I believe that was the first time I'd lifted and carried a child before and I was afraid I'd drop him.

In his room I took his shoes and coat off and put him under the covers and shut the blinds and I went into the kitchen and opened some beers.

I woke up in my bedroom a jumble of hours later. Still in my suit and shoes – I hadn't meant to fall asleep. It looked hazily late outside the window. And it was, it was around 8 o'clock. I fretted about Caspar and I went through to his room to see him. He was still asleep.

In the kitchen I made him a cheese sandwich with lots of toppings and I added a biscuit and packet of crisps and bottle of orange juice to that on a tray and I crept into his room and laid the tray on the table so he could wake up to it.

I undressed and took a shower, my body all caky from the funeral and my feet were black from the sweaty socks and I got clean. My face looked especially ugly in the mirror. *What a lousy human being I am* I thought and then I brushed my teeth and went into my bedroom to sleep again.

Caspar was already awake when I awoke in the morning. He'd turned the laptop on and was rewatching *The Simpsons*.

"Hey there kiddo," I said in the doorway, "how are you feeling?"

He didn't look at me but he dealt me a thumbs up and he hadn't done that before.

I made him some breakfast in the kitchen. Caspar came through of his own accord and sat at the table and he actually gave me a fright cos I wasn't expecting him: I looked up and he was suddenly there.

We ate at the table and my awkwardness hit me so I turned the radio on. This was the day when I would ask him who he wanted to raise him. I knew he was going to pick Kelsie. His Aunt. I had no clue how to suggest the idea.

He munched at the *Frosties*.

"Hey, Caspar?" I said. "You wanna maybe head down to the park for a walk after you've finished your cereal?"

Caspar nodded.

"You do? Great! We'll get ready after you're done then."

My plan was to suggest he go live with Kelsie on the walk. I thought maybe being outside would help him process the proposal.

It was another spectacular day and the park dazzled in glowing green. There weren't that many people about too, it being a weekday morning.

We walked down the hillside and the nettles were in full furnace and the butterflies mingled around the weeds beyond those and we got to the crystalline blue river. Through a group of rowan trees flew a magpie and I saluted it by instinct. Caspar noticed me do this. Puzzled.

"Your Dad not teach you to salute magpies when you see them, Caspar?" He looked down with a blank face. "They're special birds. You must respect them; if you don't salute a magpie when you see him, he'll give you bad luck for the day."

He didn't respond and my voice sounded pathetic.

We reached the bridge and went over that and passed this old lady walking her Labrador and it was about as big as Caspar was and it came towards him with interest and growled and I stepped in front of Caspar and the lady whistled at the dog and it immediately retreated and both parties parted ways.

Along the voyage there was this alternative path which diverted from the main one and I said to Caspar,

"You want to take this other path, little man? It goes along the river."

Yes, he nodded.

The smells of the flora were heady and dank as we descended the bankside.

Fecund June summer. A week before the solstice – right in the heart of the heartiest season. The hogweed and clover and dock leaf in abundance. And the bees and flies flirted with the water and Caspar was fascinated with the stones illuminated on the riverbed.

He touched the water with his frail fingers. And stayed there by the glittery water for some time and I watched him. Then he made a cup with his hands. And brought some up to his mouth.

And I intervened,

"No, Caspar," I said, "don't drink this water. It's not safe."

He was disappointed and bashful and he let the water drop from his hands back into the stream. But then we continued down the river. Caspar walked ahead of me with gusto.

It was odd to follow his small shape and there was this one part in the path where the land arose in a promenade. He went up the hill. And stopped. He'd obviously seen something ahead of him. I went up to him too.

He was smiling. Then he pointed down at the river and I followed his finger.

"Little waterfall," Caspar said.

Indeed. There was this glorious waterfall which dangled further downstream. It was only a yard in height and yet it must've been forming for many years and it sparkled and flowed and had its own roving colours.

"Yeah, boyo," I responded, "that's a lovely waterfall. I always liked that one."

He'd finally spoken to me!

My heart changed.

I was a mean man and here was this child who was altering me – me and my gnarly heart.

Caspar went down towards the waterfall. I pursued.

12

I didn't say anything to him about him moving away after that day.

And I was glad he was still with me in the house that night.

The next day he wanted to go back to the park, after I invited him. He said gem words like yes and please. Caspar was speaking.

"Have you ever played tennis before, Caspar?" I said to him.

"I have yeah, with Mum."

"I have some rackets in the cupboard. You wanna go play some tennis? There's a free court at the end of the park where we can play."

"Yes."

"Cool. Let's go and see what we have."

We went down to the cupboard in the middle of the corridor and when I opened it this sanguine dust fell out. I sneezed. Then found the tennis rackets which were jumbled in the corner. Caspar was peering behind me.

In front of the tennis rackets was my old football which I hadn't kicked in a long time. When I moved the rackets, the ball dribbled down and onto the floor, the way that balls magically do. And Caspar saw it.

"Football," he said, "can we take it to the park too?"

"Yes, if you like."

I thought I'd chucked this ball out a long time ago and it brought back bad vibes and I wish Caspar hadn't seen it. It was a pretty ball with a famous logo and nicely scolded with graft marks from people kicking it.

"You were a football player?" Caspar said. To me.

I turned to him.

"I was yeah."

"Can I see the ball?"

I handed it to him and he enjoyed the nylon and rubber smells of it.

"How'd you know I was a player?" I said to him.

"Dad told me."

"..."

"You played for real teams didn't you?"

"I did."

"Dad said you had to stop."

"Well yeah, eventually. I got injured. I couldn't play anymore. I didn't think Dad would tell you all of this, Caspar."

"He liked talking about you."

I was silenced. I picked the ball up along with the rackets.

"There's no point in speaking about a moany old fart like me," I said, "Let's go down to the park and we can muck around with whatever you like."

13

I could have simply left the football in the house and not taken it with us. It seemed that my life decisions were poor and that I kept making them, unwittingly; I was improvising and not creating anything good: I just didn't know it at the time.

We went to the park. And Caspar was energised with the ball. As we walked we passed it back and forth to each other.

Yes, I had the injury in my right kneecap. The famous one which had finished my career. And it actually still got sore, fifteen years after it happened. But, boo hoo, it might've been worse. I could use my left leg and foot. And it was enjoyable to feel a ball again. Nostalgic. Obviously: but I was surprised I still had the natural skill with it. The way I used to play. I didn't think – I just hit it.

"You're pretty good with a ball, Caspar," I said to him. "Have you played before?"

"Yeah. Many times with Dad."

"He never said ..." but then, why would he have? Since I barely ever spoke to him. "Did you play for any teams?"

"No."

It was a little windy today and the trees were making all kinds of nautical noises. The dandelions thrashed about in the thickets; the clouds were grey and inky and made these quick changes of tone on the land, flying about the sky.

He really was skilful with the ball and at such a young age and this got me thinking. And yet there was a great pain in watching him love it – the ball. I wasn't sure whether I loved it anymore. And of course I knew how he was feeling. Did I want to lead

Caspar into this sport? With all of its mayhem and brutality. I envied him. He was just a boy and small enough to believe in dreams.

But I was connecting with him. He had the same blood as me and he was willing to be friendly.

Caspar wore trainers and I had my 'smart-casual' ones on that I usually wore to work and they were getting all slimy with the grease of the grass from the ball.

"So you played for Rovers?" Caspar said to me, after he'd passed it back to me.

"Yes. A long time ago."

"Did you score goals?"

"Some. Ha ha. Not many."

"Dad showed me one of your goals once. You scored this cool goal for Rovers. It was on a video."

"Ho ho. I had no idea you were interested in the game, lil nephew."

"Why aren't you like a manager these days?"

"I … umm. I wouldn't be a good manager."

I kicked the ball back to him and I deliberately aimed to send it over his head to make him run away from me, and it went over him and he ran after it. For some reason I was annoyed with Tom for showing him videos of my athlete days. Maybe cos I couldn't remember any compliment from him when I was a sportsman. Why was he proudly showing his son footage of my career when he hadn't been encouraging when I was performing well? I didn't understand.

And hearing a child talk about my history like that was unprecedented. It didn't make me proud. It brought back a concoction of memories and I wasn't sure of the ingredients, of the result that they made. I hadn't expected them to come back all at once when I was a middle aged man. It's amazing how time works like that.

Caspar passed back to me with the ball. He was a far distance away and he kicked it with that level of strength and accuracy. I grinned. And caught the ball with my left foot. And half-volleyed it back to him. He had control of the ball too. Took it down on his knee. I just suspected that he had talent and that I could nurture it if I tried.

"Hey, Caspar," I called to him. "If we walk to the end of the park there are some old goalposts where you can practise shooting. I'll be goalie and you work on your shooting. Fancy that?"

"Yes please."

I was always shit as a goalie. I didn't like the ball whizzing at me at whichever hefty velocity … and this made the fact of my once being a professional soccer player all the more ironic.

We got to the goals. Nobody else was on any of the pitches and there were rugby posts too on the far end and the posts were giants and statues, these vessels to be respected. We had the whole arena to us alone and the wind flumed across the field in mad length and I had to shout across to Caspar so he could hear me.

"I'll kick the ball across to you," I yelled. "And from where it stops. You take a pop at goal. And I'll try and save it. You got me?"

He nodded. He was nervous. I kicked the first try-out to him, making sure it was inside the box. On the corner. Quite a tricky shot. Caspar prepared and took time to calculate his aim. He stepped up and smacked it and I saved it easily and he was embarrassed that he'd fluffed it.

"Not bad, Caspar," I said, "keep trying. You have

to keep going."

I rolled the ball out a little farther to the other side.

He stepped up and whacked it and I had to properly save it. It made me smile again, that he was so spirited.

"Ace effort, Caspar," I said. "Persevere with it."

We did the same again and Caspar, before he kicked, looked up at me.

"Uncle?"

"Yeah?"

"You think I could be a player one day?"

"If you work hard at it every day, then, yes."

"I want to be that. To be like you."

"You can be better than me if you put the work in."

"Will you help me?"

"Of course I will. Now, Caspar. Have a shot on goal."

PART TWO

14

I had to find Caspar a new school in the autumn following that unusual summer.

There was a primary school in our 'catchment area' but I already knew I couldn't send Caspar there. It was a bad place and he'd get torn apart there. I suppose that every school does this to kids – shreds them up – but if I sent him *there* he would just get traumatised. So I endeavoured to get him in to a school which was more middle ground.

That was a ten minute drive from my flat. I went down there and spoke to the inductee person – this rather pretty woman who was in charge of that kind of thing. Of kids who weren't in the catchment area but wanted to get in.

I felt totally out of my depth going down to this primary school and meeting people like her. Her beauty was intimidating. I'd brought school records from Caspar's previous school in order to prove that he was a bright student. And he was.

So I sat down with this dame in this small office in a school. And frankly I pitied Caspar for having to go to *any* school because I remembered what it was like in primary and high school both and I fucking hated both of them. My mission was to ensure that he wouldn't get as heavily bullied as I was. Perhaps I was being paranoid but that was my honest thinking.

"My nephew's a really clever lad," I said to her, "I'm sure he'd fit in academically. I've no doubt about that. Here: I can show you his grades from his last school."

I faffed about with the papers.

She looked over them. I couldn't tell whether she was impressed or not.

"Yes," she said eventually, "it looks like he's a good all-rounder. I can see that. But, tell me, Mr Ballard. Why are you so nervous? You seem ... angsty. How come?"

"I'd just really rather my nephew went to this school than that other one. You must get what I'm saying? He'd be safer here."

"I know what you mean ... You mentioned on the phone the other day that you were his uncle and that you'd only recently taken him in. That made me curious too?"

"Ah yeah well I would've said this on the phone. But it's quite heavy. His parents died in a car crash a few months back. So they can't take care of him any more and he's with me now."

"God."

"Uh hu."

"How has he been keeping?"

"He's a tough boy. I see resilience in him. And we're getting along okay."

"Good, good. I don't think there will be a problem with the application Mr Ballard. We have spaces. And just by his record I imagine he will be accepted by us fine."

"Thank you. For your time and everything."

Ten days later I received a letter saying that Caspar was accepted into the school and it was a great relief to me. He would start late August. I started out by buying him school uniforms and stationery and lunchboxes and so on.

Throughout that summer I had to return to work.

Couldn't survive on sick pay for eternity. So I hired a girl to come to the flat and sit Caspar in the weekdays and then I'd get home in the evenings.

She was called Katie. A university student. Extroverted and had this fantastic orange hair.

Caspar was charmed by her immediately. She made him laugh and this made me jealous because I wasn't capable of doing that – making him chuckle. But, yeah: throughout the summer she wasn't studying so she was able and willing to look after Caspar in the daytimes when I was at work. She fed and played with him and befriended him a great deal and she deserves an elite accolade in his brain development. Women are way better communicators than men. Katie will have helped his mind mature when he needed it. I paid her more than she requested because she did such a swell job with him.

There was one evening in July when I arrived home from work. I went into the flat. Katie was reading Caspar a story in the living room. I stopped in the hallway and listened to her. She had such a great thespian voice. It was just a normal accent but the way she used it in loops and bounds was mesmeric. I wished I had the talent to do that. To read to a child in that way; I'd bought Caspar all of these books but so far I hadn't braved reading them out loud to him cos I wasn't able to do that.

I did know the story. Knew the plot and the words almost verbatim. My mother used to read it to me. Katie was as fine an orator as she was.

"The end," Katie said, "would you like something to drink, Caspar?"

"I'm fine, thanks."

"K. I'm just nipping for a pee."

Katie came out of the living room. I was still in

my coat and everything when she came into the corridor. She hadn't heard me come into the flat and she yelped when she saw me. Cute yelp.

"Haha," she said, "sorry Ralph I didn't know you were there."

"I'm sorry too I should have called."

"No problem."

"You read to my nephew very well."

She winked and said, "I know I do."

Then she went into the toilet.

I was somebody that never went to university. Who had never been that attractive or charming. You must've noticed that I keep comparing myself to other people – when you barely know much about me yet?

Katie was a good soul. Much merit to her for the effort she put into Caspar during that period.

15

It was the night before Caspar's first day at his new school.

He woke me up with noise: he was crying in his room. I checked the clock and it was 3 a.m. I went through to see him.

"Caspar, buddy," I peered into the darkness, "What's wrong my friend?"

His whimpering was dangerous and contagious, angelic and hypnotic, and I had to go to him. I sat on the corner of the bed.

Caspar shivered under the covers.

"What happened lil nephew?"

"I had a bad dream."

"That's all right. We all have bad dreams. It's over now."

His body trembled under the fabric and I wanted to touch him to calm him down but didn't have the courage.

"I'm sorry you had a nightmare, lad, but it wasn't real."

"It's still sore."

"I know it is. What happened in the nightmare?"

"Mum and Dad were still alive."

"Ah."

"So it wasn't really a nightmare. I was with them. They could still talk and see me. Then I woke up and they weren't here."

"I'm so sorry, Caspar. That they aren't here for you."

It was other-worldly speaking to him in the gloom.

There was a long period of quiet whereby his body eased and he stopped shaking and yet I felt I was doing no good for him. I couldn't be a substitute for his parents.

"Anything I can do for you, Caspar?"

"I don't think so. Sorry for waking you up."

"Don't be sorry. I can make you an Ovaltine?"

"No I'm good."

"Anything else?"

"I'm fine."

I was gonna say to him 'You can come sleep with me if you like?' but this seemed super weird and it was a fleeting thought and I don't think any sane person would want to sleep next to me. So I just had to leave him by himself. Caspar was ashamed for crying in front of me. He hadn't done that in some time.

And it was a shame because he had to wake up for school in a few hours.

I shut the door on him that night after saying good night. And I knew he would have to head back into sleep, fearing that he might dream again about my brother. There was no other option than to let him deal with his grief himself. Or maybe I was too small minded to think of another way. I was a bad uncle that night. A coward. Perhaps I've never been a proper uncle at all.

16

Yes. I remember the injury that destroyed my playing career. I think about it every day. The noise in the stadium, the chanting, the assault.

That's what it was. From the other player – this beefy man a few years younger than me – he wasn't trying to tackle me. It was designed to hurt me and he succeeded and the referee saw it and knew that too and all the opponent got for it was a red card. That was it. No assault charge or ban for longer than a couple of games.

Whenever I got fouled and was knocked down I always made the point of getting up asap. I'd stand up and not winge on the floor. That night I literally couldn't get up. I tried, but my right knee wasn't working.

The incident happened right in front of the away stand and they'd seen the challenge and had loved it and cheered when the crunch occurred, and when their man got sent off they directed all their boyish hatred on me. The profanity that came out of their mouths … wow … it was prime high-school esque stupidity. They were using words like 'penis' and 'peedo'. At me … And as I waited for the stretcher I thought "Why did I ever sign myself up to this sport?" I was already used to abuse from the crowd and had hardened myself from it a long time earlier and I really wished to get up and run off and continue the game. I couldn't.

And they thought I was time wasting. They threw coins and cans, whatever they had on them. Because it was a night game they'd had a chance to get drunk before the match and they were losing 3 – 1 and I'd assisted one of the goals.

The medics came on and looked at my kneecap. I'd barely ever been injured before and was lucky enough to have a naturally healthy, tough physique. One of the medic men (Paulie) looked at my kneecap and his face turned grim.

"Oh, shit, Ralph," he said. When he said that I knew this was something different. Ominous.

And obviously it was just so fucking painful. I mean ... have you ever been knocked on the kneecap? Even lightly?

My fans (the Home fans) applauded me when I was lifted off the pitch and it was the final time I ever heard them do that. The medics wheeled me into the hub of the stadium. And the sound of the fans and commotion of the game lessened in a diminuendo ... all the rash noise died away as they moved me down these corridors towards the medical room. Where they examined me very briefly. Until Paulie said,

"I think we need to get you to a hospital, son."

I said I didn't want to go in an ambulance. They protested. I dunno – I just hated the idea of being put in an ambulance. So they drove me there instead. And helped me limp into the building.

It's amazing how physical pain can alter one's perspective and make you appreciate things you'd shrugged off beforehand when you were all healthy. Paulie and Chris, the physios that night. I'd never spoken to them much and had always pretentiously thought of them as being a bit thick and plebian. Now I was relying on them for support. And realised how dismissive I'd been of them and it took a broken kneecap to make such a simple realisation:

I wasn't a great football player, was not as good as I thought I was. I was five months off my 30th birthday and should have been in the peak of my career. This wasn't accurate. Rovers had released me two years back. And my new club was my way of reviving my talent ... reviving what was possibly never there.

"What you looking so glum about, champ?" Paulie said.

"My knee fucking hurts."

He and Chris laughed.

"Don't worry sonny you're gonna be fine."

"I don't think I will, Paulie. I think this is a bad one. And that bastard who did it. He meant it."

"He got dismissed, man. Everybody knows he's a dirty player. He's a nobody."

"What if he's ruined me though?"

"He hasn't ruined you. Come on Ralphie don't be a baby. We'll see what the docs say."

This was back in the days when smaller football teams weren't willing to pay for costly private medical treatment. Plus, it would've taken six months for the breakage to mend on its own. And then I was a thirty year old winger without a club. Yeah it was brutal as hell. And my drinking worsened after that.

I'd already had a history with beer but those six months out I just drank and drank to harm myself. I was furious that my career hadn't gone the way I wanted it. I'd wallow and weep. Christ, I was a wreck.

During the same period I was still planning a comeback in my mind. *I'm still only thirty. I could play for another four years or so. Even if it's with a smaller club. Can still contribute to a team.* Everybody likes those comeback stories, the romantic resurgence of a sportsman. We like those household names and telling their stories of redemption.

I wasn't doing anything to aid my kneecap and six months of drinking turned into one year. After that I did tone it down. I went to see a physiotherapist. I turned 31. The physiotherapist said that I could technically play if I were to wise up with my diet. But she said that there was severe damage to the knee and that an injury could easily happen again if I decided to return.

That was in the early summer. When the new transfer market was picking up and clubs were looking for players.

I met up with my agent. In order to help me find a new club.

For some reason I thought the meeting with him went well. He seemed enthusiastic about getting me somewhere. It was my inability to read cues off of people well that masked my analysis of the situation.

He rejected me as a client after that meeting. In quite the petulant way. He just stopped responding to my phonecalls and then he got his receptionist to send me an email telling me that he was no longer interested in representing me.

Do you find this narrative miserable? Aye. I've never told anybody about this. Never had the courage to go to a therapist or something similar. I wouldn't belong in a counsellor's room. Just give up reading if you find me boring or negative. But know that there are positive bits to come. I've done a few decent things with my days. It's not all bleak. Have trust, if you want to.

When I was 31 it all came to a climax. My problems I mean.

My drinking wasn't a social thing by any means. I didn't go to pubs. In fact I hated pub atmospheres and avoided them. What I did do when I was drunk was go for walks in the evenings with my headphones on. As a kind of therapy – I'd walk about the city and would be out for hours just wandering about.

I took beers with me in my bag and drank them along the way.

Why don't I find a new agent and try again with a new club? I know I could play for anybody if I really put my mind to it and I can knock off this blooming drinking. You can do it, Ralph. You know you can.

Those sentences were going through my mind when I turned down a new street.

A group of lads were coming up towards me. They were drunk as well. They were all primmed up in night-out gear and they were singing. Three of them.

They all went quiet when they saw me.

I felt their eyes on me. And I thought about retreating and turning down the side street next to me to head away from them … but if I did that then it would be a show of cowardice and they might chase me, so I kept walking.

We came within maybe fifteen yards of one another. I wasn't looking at them directly, only in my peripheral vision. I sussed they were in their early twenties. Young enough for alcohol to make them barbaric.

"That's Ballard," I heard one of them proclaim.

They stopped. And I kept walking and tried not to show I was quickening the pace.

"Ralph Ballard," I heard behind me, "that's him isn't it?"

"He played for Rovers."

Then they followed me and called after me and I tried to ignore them.

"Hey, you," they called and I finally turned around.

(The street was deserted. All shut-for-the-night department stores. There were CCTV cameras on the corners of them but what could they do to help me in the present moment?)

I wanted to run properly now but if I did this then they would definitely attack.

They were ugly lads. One of them was like six foot four. Sports clothes. Smells of aftershave and vodka.

"You're Ralphie Ballard aren't you?"

"You know I am."

"You played for Rovers."

"Uh hu."

"He *used* to. He got sold because he was shit."

They guffawed hahahahaha in raging tandem. I walked on.

"Hold on a sec, Ralph. Wait there."

"Would you boys just leave me alone?"

"No need to get aggressive, man. We just want to speak to you."

They came closer and they formed a semi circle around me and I got the hunch that they'd done this type of thing before. That they were out specifically to do this kind of thing.

"Who you playing for now?" the main one said. The 6"4 chap. He was blonde and his eyes were bloodshot.

"As in a football club?" I said. "I don't have one."

"Yeah," one of the other ones intervened, "he got injured."

"He got fucked on the pitch. The other boy did his

kneecap in."

And they all did their ha ha guffawing again.

I moved on from them.

"Come back, Ballard."

I didn't stop.

So the main big blonde guy ran after me and he grabbed my shoulder. I flinched and recoiled. He took exception to my reaction. And he punched me. In the cheekbone. I thought, *why not just go for it*, and I smacked him under the chin. He fell over quite tremendously.

But then his buddies rushed me. They tackled me down. I hit the concrete and then they started pummelling me and then blonde big guy joined in.

I remember being kicked in the stomach. And the wind went out of me. I needed to vomit and breathe at the same time and my whole torso wasn't working.

Then one of them said,

"I'm gonna take a penalty kick at his head," and them all laughing.

And his shape darted towards me and then I blanked out.

17

I woke up on the street some time later. Having no clue how I got there. And it took me a while to recall what had happened.

Ah yeah, I got jumped ... battered. I checked my pockets and I was surprised that they hadn't mugged me as well. My wallet and phone and keys were all still there. So they just wanted to nail me. They certainly succeeding with that.

I stood up. Dizzy. And this intense swelling came in my stomach and I needed to sit back down again. It built and built, this sensation in my gullet, and I couldn't repeal it ... and threw up all over the street. And got down on the knees again and I retched and retched.

It was nearly five in the morning. And the vomit frothed in the dawn light and I wondered what on earth I was doing with my life, it was all so ludicrous.

I shivered and shuddered. It was the coldest I've ever felt. And it was a lucky thing to have woken up when I did.

It seemed like being beaten up was my fault. I didn't go to the police or the hospital, even though I was concussed, and I should have done. When I got back home my face was all puffy and there were bruises all over my body ... but it seemed like it was my doing that it all happened.

I knew violence from high school. Violence, to males, is quite a difficult thing to understand unless it's happened to you personally. I often regurgitate violence and nurture it in my most despondent periods. The rage never goes anywhere.

That morning when I got my head kicked in and was battered unconscious, was my lowest moment. I could only ascend or degenerate following that.

18

Caspar finished his first day of school and I drove down to the institution to pick him up. I waited outside my car close to the building. The school bell rang its demented shrill noise. Then all of these kids milled out. God, I felt so bad for them. Most of them were bigger than Caspar and they were all joyous to be unleashed.

I waited five minutes and he hadn't showed yet and I was panicking ... but then he appeared. Caspar had this terrific curly hair. He came into the sunlight and saw me and he grinned. I went towards him and hugged him and he held me back.

"How was your first day, son?"

"It was fine. Was fine."

"Excellent. Come on. I'll drive you back home and we can have some dinner. Anything you like."

We drove home and I asked him a few questions. Like, what his teacher was like? Did he meet any cool other kids? That sort of thing. He was airy in his answers. It was a lot to handle for him. When we got in I offered him all kinds of meals, takeaways, anything.

"Uncle Ralph?" he said.

"Yeah?"

"Can we go out to the park before we eat?"

"Of course we can."

"Yes, sure."

"I'd like to play some football."

That evening it was wispy with rain and fleeting with patches of sun. We went down to the park and I let him practise with his shooting again. During the summer I'd bought him a pair of boots. And he liked to wear a Rovers top, which I'd also gotten him.

I remember this one brilliant bit:

Where I kicked the ball outside of the box. To try and challenge him. Make it difficult for him to see what he would do ... and he positioned himself before the ball and took a long time to hit. Then he whacked it. And I didn't try to save it. It seemed to forever stay in the air and we both watched it sink and sink towards the goal. It panged off the crossbar. With this wonderful sound. We looked at each other. Then burst out laughing. We giggled for minutes, the moment was that fine.

It was with this that I thought *I'm gonna try and make this kid a proper athlete and I don't care whether he's better than me. I want him to be.*

But that autumn was quite a serene period, surprisingly. Caspar settled into his new school and wasn't having any difficulties.

He wanted to go to the park almost every evening and the autumn brought the cold and the cold brought the leaves and they filled up the grass in their glorious dead colours. We couldn't play so long unto the evening because the nights were shortening. Caspar was sad when he had to go home.

In early October there came my first parent's evening. I wasn't even a parent. They were brutally aware of that when I went down to the school to meet up with the teachers. I'd asked Katie to sit Caspar that night.

I felt as out of place as I usually did. The parent's night partook in the gym hall and the teachers would sit around these desks with name placards and the name I was looking out for was MRS WRIGHT ...

and I saw this placard with that on it and came up to this blonde haired woman. She gave me a clammy handshake. And was very nervous when I sat down to speak to her.

"So how's Caspar doing in general?" I said.

"He's doing more than fine," Mrs Wright said. She fumbled with some sheets of paper and showed me the marks on the report card, "these are exceptional results. He's a clever boy."

"Yeah that's ace stuff. I knew he would do well. He has courage."

"There's one thing I have to bring up, Mr Ballard?"

"Okay?"

"I understand that he had a family bereavement?"

"Yes, he did."

"..."

"Yeah – you already know the details of that. You're his teacher."

"So how's he coping with that?"

"He's a wee boy and he's doing remarkably well with it. He's dealing with it better than I am."

"Right ... It's just that ... umm, there's a social issue with him in the classroom."

"What kind of issue?"

"He doesn't talk to the other children."

"So what is the problem?"

"He's not interested in the other kids. Doesn't speak to them."

"Does this affect his grades?"

"Well ... no. It's just that. Emm. Maybe Caspar needs to go to a counsellor or something like that?"

"Why?"

"You *know* why. He is so uncommunicative. He plays by himself in the playground and has no interest in the other children."

"Well what does he do in the playground?"

"He just mucks about with his football."

"Why is this a bad thing?"

"I'm just worried about his social development, is all. If he doesn't have friends then he won't develop as an adult."

"Do you have any degree in psychology Mrs Wright?"

"Sorry?"

"Do you have any proper psychological know-how? Have any degree in that specific field?"

"I don't. But I'm a concerned teacher who cares about this boy who obviously has some problems."

"He's traumatised. But he's dealing with it in his own way. And he'll be fine. He's dealing with it better than you are as well."

I was burning in the face. And there were people at the other desks who were watching us. Mrs Wright was afraid.

"Sorry," I said, "I just get emotional when talking about him. Didn't mean to get angry."

"It's all right," she said.

"How's he doing in PE?"

"Pardon?"

"How is Caspar doing in PE?"

"He's great at that."

"Does the school have a football team? I should have enquired before."

"It does have a team yeah. But not for kids as young as Caspar."

"He's very good. I think he could join the team. How old do you have to be to join the team?"

"Umm well I think the team that we have are nine or ten. Maybe he is a bit too young. But I'm not sure."

"He is young but I'm sure he can fit in. Can Caspar do a trial? Who's the coach of the team?"

"That would be Mr Crandles."

"Is he here tonight? In this hall?"

"No he's not here tonight but I can put you in contact with him?"

"Please."

"Mr Crandles is a nice guy," she wrote down the room number of his office. "I don't know his exact number off hand but if you go there to that room you can speak to him. He'll help you out."

"Thanks a lot."

That meeting with Mrs Wright brought back a fable from my school days. When the atmosphere was far different. This would've been when I was about Caspar's age in this part of the book, so six or seven. There's a bit of background to this tale and it'll seem a bit wacky but here it goes.

One spring when I was a schoolboy there was a game going around the boys. It was like a 'cruel trick' game. Whereby a boy would come up to you (it didn't matter if he was a mate or enemy) and say this line to you. If you were too slow to react, then he'd thump you in the balls. This was basically the intelligence of the game ... umm. Aye, and the verbal line was something like, "Always keep your baw space safe."

But anyway I was one of the lads who was too tardy to realise the threat and protect my testicles and then this other lad whacked me in them. Ah yes, the male pain. You can't really appreciate it unless you're male. And I went to the toilet with this guttural agony throughout my torso. Then the bell screamed and I had to go back to class.

I thought it was a standard knock in the nuts and that I would get over it. I didn't. Couldn't concentrate in maths class, or physics after that. The two subjects I hated most. My nuts felt like they were on fire.

At the end of the day I walked home and sweated crazily the whole way. When I got in my mother was there. She sensed something was wrong. I had to confess to her what had happened. She took me into our bathroom and I had to pull my trousers and boxers down and show her my genitals. She was embarrassed as well. But she took a look at what had happened and then took me to the hospital.

One of my testicles had been twisted around within the sack. If you get me? The smack from earlier had spun it around on its, ehh, organic string or whatever the technical term is. And, in this state my nut was losing oxygen and would have to be untwisted or else it would perish inside my sack and become diseased.

They told me this several hours after being in the hospital, us having been lounging in the waiting room. My mother was incredibly irritated and didn't want to be there; she wanted to be at home, drinking. (At one point she said to me, as we were waiting for a nurse to examine me, "Why did you let somebody *hit* you! How could you be so careless?")

I didn't fully comprehend what was happening because I was that young and then suddenly it was decided I was going to have an operation. The doctor was this foreign chap with a beard and when he said the word operation I started crying and mother was humiliated that I wept in front of him.

"Don't worry," the foreign doctor said to me and then he walked out of the room and I didn't see him again.

"Are you crying because it's sore or because you're worried?" mother said to me.

She did respond but my memory didn't chronicle the words.

Within an hour I was in an Operating Room surrounded by adults draped in scrubs looking at me.

They had to knock me out and so they put a mask up to my face. They told me it takes up to ten seconds for the vapour to knock a person out and they told me to count. And suddenly this wonderful flowery air was flowing through my mouth and into my head and

I counted to three seconds. I smiled. And everybody in the room laughed. Then I switched off.

So they operated on me and cut my nut sack open and turned my testicle around to its original posture and then sealed the sack back up again. Ha.

I woke up fairly quickly afterwards and I was being trolleyed through a new section of the hospital. I remember this tiny mark of blood on my cloth. Duvet, rather. It was odd to know that it was my blood and yet it wasn't scary or brave, only a fact.

It was mandatory for me to stay over in the hospital for one night. The nurses were nice and had that effeminate niceness which only women can fool kids with. Women can fool you that they're genuine even if they aren't. One of them brought me some buttered toast. I remember the spasm of salt from the butter on my tastebuds. Then another nurse came and gave me an injection of something and I do not know what I was injected with. It took her a while to insert the needle and there was this bright second of pain and she breathed heavily and was overweight and jolly and her own arms were profoundly veiny.

That night before I went to bed they showed me a VHS of *Tom & Jerry* and it made it me giggle with all of its multicoloured mania.

Then when the night continued they turned the lights off and it was peculiar to be in this long room with all of these strangers in the other beds … but I was tired and didn't feel threatened and I fell asleep.

In the morning my Dad came to pick me up. I was to be discharged today. He took me down to the toilet at the end of the corridor, where I was supposed to pee. I went into the cubicle and peed.

"Is your wound seeping?" he called over the door.

"Huh?"

"The nurses told me to ask you about your wound, down there. Is it seeping?"

"I don't really want to look at it."

"Okay."

And so the nurse had to take a look at it later in the day. She pulled the blinds around my bed. Saw it and saw that nothing was wrong and then gave me the okay to go home.

And I went back home with my Dad in a taxi and he was gruff and embarrassed as well and it felt like he was doing his duty.

I didn't have this atrocious pain in my genitals anymore and that was the good thing. As well as having a few days off school. It was a lil holiday. I'd survived. My parents were kind and helped me out with meals and so on. They did well.

Then I had to go back to school. In the new week.

And do you know who I think it was that told everybody? It was Tom. My wee brother.

It might've just been one person. One other boy who he told but it was obviously him that did it. He snitched me out. That I'd been on a hospital for an operation on my balls.

The instant I got back to school they all ripped the fuck out of me. Somewhere throughout the gossip the information had been skewed. And for a while they thought I'd gotten one of my balls removed during the op.

And they picked up on that famous Adolph Hitler

song. You know it, right? "Hitler, he's only got one ball. The other is in the Albert Hall." And they replaced my name with it. "Ralphie. He's only got ..." and so on and so forth. Whenever we were out of teacher earshot they all sang along – it was mass hysteria.

I would never have told any of the school clan that I'd been in the hospital for a genital thing. Because I knew they would do what they did if they found out. The shouting and giggling. They even tried to smack me in the nuts again. More than once. Just to reopen the wound because they found it amusing. I didn't let them. Children can be rife cunts, can't they?

Tom was the one who told them. I never asked him to admit it. Who wouldn't have admitted it. I'm still angry with him for that. I don't see why I should forgive him for that. They sang that rollicking song to me for weeks and months.

I have this purple scar on my scrotum from that operation. It's a messy sight indeed.

There was an add-on tale in my adolescent years when I went to the hospital again cos I felt a lump in my scrotum. Thought it was testicular cancer.

So I went and got a screening. This man put some gel on my nuts and wavered about with this machine thing.

"Yes, that's a cyst," he said, looking at the screen.

And I thought he meant that I had cancer. But then he said,

"It's nothing cancerous. It will be a mark from your previous operation. Nothing to worry about. You're all clear."

Aye so that's a glimpse of my medical history. How

does this example connect with my meeting with Mrs Wright, as a man? What's the relation between the memories?

The bullying with the testicle thing really turned me sullen. The length of time and the betrayal from my sibling. I went dark. Got more aggressive than I already was. It actually helped to be aggressive because the boys didn't fuck with me if I showed it.

I shielded myself from people. I think I just lost faith in good people after that. Because I actually had a band of mates before the whole balls thing. I remember seeing them in the playground singing along with all of the others ... their shiny teeth, their sadistic eyes. I'm not even exaggerating.

It was mandatory for me to go to school. I turned up. Made an effort not to speak to anybody unless it was a teacher who would thrash me unless I didn't respond. I didn't speak to the family either. What was the point? What did they care?

I shut off and stayed in my room a lot and read lots of books. I'd keep the curtains shut constantly. My mind functioned better in the dark. I just hated the sounds of other people.

Then I cut myself one night. I had this rosy Swiss Army Knife that my Grandad had given me for Christmas.

I don't know why I cut myself: it just happened. It was on my left forearm and the slash was bad and I tried to disguise it from my mother in the morning. But she saw it. And freaked. She treated it with this brown liquor stuff she had in her nursey belongings and she put a bandage over it. She said to me,

"Don't do this again, Ralph."

"Okay, I won't."

"And don't tell your Dad that you did this."

"Right."

"I'm going to take you to see somebody soon. It will be all right."

I had no clue what she meant but I just said that that was fine.

Mother took me to see a psychotherapist a few days later. I didn't know what a psychotherapist was. Or why I was in this brown warm room with this strange silver haired man who was only speaking to my mother and not me. She narrated to him.

"He barely ever makes eye contact. He can't make any friends. They mock him at school. I'm embarrassed to have the family around him at Easter, Christmas, whatever. He just doesn't talk. He doesn't have any social skills. And now he's cutting himself."

"How bad was the cut?" this man said to her.

"It was treatable, but serious. I don't want that to happen again."

"Has he tried suicide before?"

"Oh, no. Thank god."

"Hmm."

They continued speaking about me in the third person for several minutes. It was terrifying. Bewildering. Mad.

The white haired man hadn't addressed me once throughout the entire meeting. Then he finally turned to me and said,

"You aren't going to hurt yourself again, are you,

my friend?"

"No."

"And you aren't going to hurt anybody else?"

"No, I won't. Why would I do that?"

"Okay," and then he turned back to my mother and said, "I think I have an idea of what this is. I'd like to give your son a few tests. Just to check a few things."

"What kind of tests?" my mother said nervously.

"Nothing physically. Some paperwork for him to fill out. It's nothing to fret over. I just want to check up some details."

Mother nodded uncertainly. The therapist man told me to leave the room while he prepared some paperwork. And he wanted to say a few things to mother one on one.

Then I was in a new room with these papers. My mother gave me a pen and left me with them in this strange room.

Questionnaires. Indexes and numbers. Black ink.

It was like taking exams which I hadn't prepared for and I still had zilch clue what was happening or why my mother had brought me here.

The questionnaires I found erratic;

'Do you find it hard to get dressed in the morning?'

'Do you struggle to make yourself a meal?'

'Is it tricky to complete tasks?'

'Is it difficult to concentrate on tasks for a long time?'

I ticked no for all of them. The questions were insulting and I ticked the NO boxes again and again for that reason. I just couldn't relate to the content.

The bulk of those questions came in one grey-papered form. Then I moved onto another form of yellow paper which was in a matrix style where I would rank the answer according to 'strongly disagree', 'slightly disagree', 'slightly agree' and 'strongly agree'. The queries were more intimate. Yet baffling in a different way;

'Do you often hear small noises when other people do not?'

I ticked strongly agree for that one.

'Is it difficult to understand somebody just from their facial expression alone?'

I ticked slightly agree for that one.

'When you're reading a story is it hard to work out a character's intentions?"

I slightly disagreed with that.

'Would you rather go to a party or a library?'

This was the killer one. I was only a kid but it still seemed absurd and dodgy. I smirked. I considered my experiences of parties and libraries up until that point in my six/seven years on the planet.

Parties. Well, I'd been invited to a few disco parties by school'mates'. The kids were all fucked up on soda and gelatine sweets and they listened to shit music in a rented-out venue and I didn't want to speak to any of them. And festivities at home consisted of mother inviting the extended family around at Christmas, being bludgeoned drunk and my father being silently afraid of her. She fell about, literally, and it made me angsty that she might injure herself. (This happened a fair number of times. Her falling over. Tripping down the stairs – that kinda thing.) If that's what parties were then I wasn't particularly fond.

What about libraries? Well there was one in the school and I often went in there during the lunchbreak. It was a sleepy place and the librarian was fat and old and miserable, but she was nice to me. I read these fantasy books I was keen on – a series of them. For some reason I was too scared to actually lend them out and I wasn't a fast reader at that stage and so I just read chapters in snippets in the library. Until the librarian (her name was Mrs Wren) said one afternoon, "You can take it home with you if you like," and she showed me how to borrow a book.

And my mother would take me up to the local library on the occasional Saturday. (I feel I should give this woman ((mother)), the person that bore me, some credit: most of what I've said about her thus far has been negative.) And they had that same series of fantasy books in there too and I went through them with relish. They were illustrated too. With these wacky drawings of creatures and gowned men, wizards and magic, and a lot of it was enticingly violent and I admit I liked it, for some reason, even though it was disturbing.

Comparing parties to libraries was a joke. I'd never even experienced alcohol yet, nor got why my mother abused it so heavily. But, obviously, I cannot judge her these days, having fallen into that same murky condition myself.

So, to the question of whether I'd rather head to a party than library, I chose strongly disagree.

And then just as I was about to go on to the next question, the door opened.

The silver fox mental doctor was in the doorway.

"You finished yet, son?" His smile was very fake. He was agitated.

"I finished one of them but I'm still doing this one."

"How much of it have you completed?"

"Ehh … I'm on page three."

"That's fine that should be enough. You've been in here a long time. Your Mum's waiting on you. And I have to see other patients soon."

He came towards me and took my forms, the finished one and unfinished one and then left the room without a word. He didn't shut the door and he walked back into the office, where my mother was still sitting. Then closed his office door.

I crept up to my door and hovered in the hallway. It was an alien place. I knew I shouldn't creep up to office door but I wanted to hear what they were saying. The door was thick and the voices muffled and I couldn't discern the exact words; the therapist was doing most of the speaking.

A child often thinks he has committed some crime, when he or she hasn't, and that's what I thought I had done that day. I imagined that mother would take me somewhere else next after the doctor gave his analysis. That I would be made to do further tests. All kinds of crazy imaginations flumed in me. I shook and tapped my feet. Then I heard my mother's voice in a crescendo – she got all loud. And I thought this was the catalyst of my fears. There came a commotion in the room and rumbling on the floor.

So I ran back to my test room and hid inside. I sat back at my desk to pretend that I hadn't left the seat.

Mother stormed out of the office. And called my name.

"Ralph! Come here."

I ran back to her. Her cheeks were red and eyeballs teary.

"We're going home now. Move." And she pushed me in the back to jolt me forward.

"What's wrong?" I said to her.

"Nothing."

"Did I do something wrong?"

"No. Hush up now."

The therapist called something from his office. He called to mother and I turned to him. She clutched my face and thrust it the other way … and I never caught what he said. There was this final image of his frame in the doorway, looking as if he might run after us. And then my mother and I were in a new corridor and on our way out of the building.

My mother was wearing her dress and her good shoes and she angrily clopped into the square outside and her soles made these pack pack pack noises on the concrete.

"I don't understand what's happened?" I said to her.

"Just come along with me Ralph. Stop asking questions."

She was icily furious the whole way home on the bus. And did not utter a word. My mother wore this specific type of perfume. Old fashioned. Synthetic flower perfume and sitting next to her on the hot bus the smell was extreme.

When we got inside the house she told me to go upstairs and stay in my room and I obeyed.

I went upstairs and Tom was ogling me curiously from his open bedroom door. He knew that she had taken me to see a 'specialist'. I thought he would make fun of me. But when I was his face he was worried.

"Just leave me alone, Tom," I said to him, and I went into my room and shut the door.

My Dad arrived home later that evening. And I heard

him go into the kitchen and speak to mother for a long while. Once again, I knew there was dialogue but I could not pick out the words.

I wasn't invited down for dinner. Tom was, but not me. And the order from mother was still in place for me to not leave the room. So I had to sneak to the toilet to take a piss whilst they were eating downstairs. When I got back into my bedroom I was just so tired and I crumpled on my bed and fell asleep.

The next day I was still scared of what mother might say to me. Whether I was in trouble.

I met her in the kitchen. She was making soup. Slashing vegetables.

"Hey Mum," I said.

"Hello Ralph."

"Everything okay?"

"Of course."

"…"

She cut the celery with graceful violence.

"Are you still angry with me?"

"When was I angry with you?"

"I thought you were yesterday."

She continued chopping and I thought about trying another question but this never came out.

I was reluctant to go further and didn't have the courage. So I left the kitchen and went upstairs again, and mother didn't say anything about the therapist visit. She went dark on it and refused to open up. To this day I still can't figure out what happened with all of that. My child brain was never able to dissect what occurred and my adult brain can't either. Hey ho.

20

It was important to get in touch with this Mr Crandles character. The coach of the kids' football team that Mrs Wright told me about. Wanted to get my nephew in a team.

I drove down to the school one afternoon and went through the building looking for the room number Wright had given me. It felt dodgy to be in a school again: felt like I wasn't supposed to be there. Most of the kids were in their classrooms cos I'd gone bang on in the daytime. I didn't even know whether this man would be in his office. But yeah I felt like a criminal. That somebody would stop me any second, worried that I was gonna shoot this place up.

There was his door and I knocked on it.

"Yeah? Who's there?" a voice called.

I opened the door and I met this bald man who was eating a sandwich in a small room.

"Hi there, is that a Mr Crandles?"

"Yes."

I felt mean for interrupting his lunch.

"I'm the guardian of one of the pupils. A boy. His name is Caspar ... They told me you were the football coach?"

"I am yeah."

"I think my boy would fit in your team well."

"Come in, sir. Close the door."

He put his plate away and got up from his chair and came across and offered me a handshake. His eyes were fierce. I mumbled my name.

"I didn't mean to bother you while you were eating," I said, "sorry about that."

"No, no, it's al good. So tell me which boy you're on about."

And he invited me the other side of his desk and I sat down.

"Caspar Ballard."

"I don't think I've met him before – the name rings no bells."

"He's young. He's only in P2."

"Okay, that will be why."

"He'll turn seven next month. Listen, coach. I think my nephew has got something. I'd like to give him an avenue to expand. Is there a chance to give him a trial for the team?"

"I thought he was your son?"

"Nephew."

"Right. What's up with you Mr Ballard? You seem terribly agitated."

"I just know I have to do this for my nephew is all."

"Well there are training sessions for the team on Wednesday nights. In the playing fields outside of the school."

"Wednesdays?"

"Yes."

"So I can bring him along tomorrow night?"

"Sure. How big is he?"

"He's average height for his age."

"K. 7 o'clock on the playing fields tomorrow. Bring the boy along. We'll see if he has any skills."

21

I took Caspar down to the fields the next evening. He was full of courage and I admired it. I made the effort to go there early and I met with Mr Crandles and these two other chaps around my age and we shook hands. They were simple guys; all of us were.

Because it was October the nights were small and there was only one floodlit Velcro pitch for the kids to train on. We were a small nation with no historical prowess in the sport.

Then the other kids started arriving. Most of them were in packs, of boys. They watched Caspar. Some of them arrived with their fathers and their fathers looked at *me* for long glances. I didn't get why they were staring.

So about thirty people were in the arena. The boys slipped their outer clothes off, got into shorts and strips and they put their boots on. Caspar was already kitted up.

I went up to Mr Crandles.

"So how does a typical training session normally work?"

"Physical training for one hour. Then we give them a game at the end."

"That's it?"

"Yeah."

And then Crandles walked away from me. Onto the Velcro pitch. And the boys started following him.

I caught up with Caspar. I bent down to him. He was smart in his gear.

"Caspar," I said, "you're gonna be tested physically for the first part. Just follow what the coaches say. And then at the end you'll have a match. I want you to go forward as much as you can. Play your best. Show then what you know you can do. You get me?"

He nodded.

"On you go boy."

I hung on the periphery whilst the boys trained and the coaches barked orders. Got them to run through the cones and whatnot. Sparky running.

Caspar dealt with it better than I thought he would. He was way skinnier than the rest of the boys but he had spirit. The other lads were dubious of him because he was a rookie.

Then all of that stuff finished and the match at the end began.

Caspar set up one goal and scored another.

Crandles told me after the game that he wanted my nephew in his team from now on.

22

That night when he played and scored his first goal and got in to the team was the first time I felt that I was succeeding as an uncle. I was so chuffed for him. And that was new for me as well: taking pleasure in somebody else being happy. And he was – he was so elated after the game. Spoke to me more warmly then ever on the ride back home.

Caspar was who brought me back to football again. I thought I'd rejected it bitterly: left it in the past. And did not expect that it would ever return … but here it was pacing in my blood again. For a long chunk of my life it'd lain dormant.

Football practise was once a week on the Wednesdays and after that first glorious occasion Caspar was addicted and wanted me to play with him in the park as often as he could. It was great to see him so animated.

On one of those evenings (in the park) I got speaking to him as we pinged the ball about.

"Caspar. It's your birthday in a few weeks' time. Is there anything special you'd like for it? Or anything you'd like to do?"

"Hmm."

He paused with the ball and got all serious.

"You don't have to come up with an answer right now," I said. "Just any time."

"Can we maybe go to a Rovers game?"

"That's what you want to do? That all? We can do something else."

"It's just that I've never been to a Rovers game before. In the stadium I mean."

"Never?"

"Nope."

I was gonna say 'You're Dad never took you to a single game!' but clamped this sentence because it was mean.

"Well, yeah, sure, I can take you to a game soon if that's really what you wanna do."

"Yes please."

"Sound well when we get home I'll look at the fixtures and get some tickets."

When we got back I looked up the fixtures on the Rovers website.

(Rovers were another thing which I had assumed I had banished in history and had vowed never to return there. In fact, I hadn't even been near the stadium since they sold me when I was 27. That was among the most gutting moments ever for me, when I learned they were rejecting me. Rovers were my boyhood club and once very special to me. And I was uneasy about going back in the present era for these reasons. But if Caspar wanted to then I could help out and omit my reservations.)

The club itself were now in the second division and had been for years and I barely followed the results in the paper anymore because there was little point.

On the coming Sunday they were playing another equally-mediocre team (Athletic) at the Rovers stadium who were lower than Rovers in the league. I thought it'd be nice for Caspar's virgin match to be a victory. So I bought some tickets online. Even Caspar's ticket was crazily overpriced. I told Caspar we'd be heading there in a few days and he was excited. I was glad for him but not for me and I went to sleep that night in a conflicted state, wondering what it would be like to go back to an institution which had abandoned me.

It was a peppery morning that Sunday and the roads when we walked down them were sparkly and silver. We got the bus into the heart of town (East side, working class district, old tenement housing) and along the streets we say the fans with the blue & red strips and scarves. Alighting from the bus we walked through the roads and the fans were singing and already a bit drunk despite it being a 12 o'clock kick-off game. Police vans milled about.

Then we veered the bend in the road and in the distance I saw the turrets of the stadium and this hollow yearning destroyed feeling crossed in my stomach and I gazed at it like an ex lover, like something which cannot die and you cannot emit from your memory and I suddenly felt far older and unaccomplished ... that I could have been a champion for this club and did have that chance ... but I never had the gall or natural ability to do that.

But I had to crush this emotional garble away. It was Caspar's day and not mine and it was wrong to be selfish and despondent around him.

So I took him to the Club Shop and I bought him his first Rover's scarf and a hat too. Then we walked up to the stands. And went through the scary turnstiles which were worn and a bit rusty and unchanged from my days and I thought they would've changed them by now but apparently not. Then we were inside the interior with thousands of other people and I got some chips and a coke for Caspar and we went out into the exterior and beheld the spanning visions of the stadium. We found our seats.

The seats filled up all around us.

Kick off was emerging and then the players were set to come out. When they did, I said to Caspar,

"Now we stand up and cheer our players, kiddo."

He did so.

Just before kick off a group of lads nearby us started up a song to jolt the mood. Caspar didn't know the words. So I sang along with them to try and teach him it. The game started.

Athletic were playing in orange and they scored in the 3rd minute. The goal came right in front of their fans – about three hundred men and boys that'd made the coach trip from their small town somewhere else in the nation – and they all went psychopathic with glee.

Caspar looked at me.

"It's all right boyo," I said. "We'll get one back on them."

Rovers didn't. My nephew and I sat through an incredibly dull first half where nothing else happened.

There was a man who was sitting a few rows behind us. Drunk. And he was pissed off that the team were doing poorly. And he kept shouting out these orders to the Rovers players, and profanities to the Athletic squad. At loud volume; a vocabulary of bastard and fucker and cunt and there was a racial slight in there as well because one of the Athletic men was black. (Two of our squad were black as well, but he said it anyway.)

I wanted to stand up and go and speak to him and ask politely if he would stop using this language in front of my kid. But he'd obviously been drinking too. He'd probably take it out on me if I did that.

So instead, when half time came, I moved Caspar

and I to another place in the stadium and we adopted these empty seats (of which there were many). And waited for the game to restart. When it did, Rovers actually did pretty well and the manager must've made some gusto speech in the dressing room because they were properly attacking the Athletic goalie. It looked like we were going to equalise and Caspar was thrilled.

One of the players got fouled and the game was stopped.

From behind me there was a tapping on my shoulder. It made me flinch. I turned. There was this older chap smiling at me.

"Excuse me?" he said. He was sitting on his own. This normal small chap with a wrinkled forehead. "I think I recognise you. You're Ralph Ballard, aren't you?"

"Yes, I am."

He offered a handshake and I took it warmly and Caspar was looking at me too.

"Rovers legend," the man said. "I remember watching you play."

"Haha. Thanks. I wasn't much of a legend."

"You are, in my book. You scored that beast of a goal ... against, umm ..."

"United?"

"Yeah! The volley! That's one of the best goals."

"I've seen that goal too," Caspar jumped in, "Ralph is my uncle!"

"That's cool, that's cool. Nice to meet you my friends."

I grew hot in the neck. Shook hands with the man again and then the game underneath us intensified and so it took the attention away from me. There was a freekick for Rovers outside of the box and our star man had it in his sights and he took a pop and it missed by a yard and the whole crowd went ohhhhh and clapped.

Rovers tried gallantly for a goal.

Up until the 80th minute. When Athletic scored a second goal, and it was a fantastic effort too – their striker chipped our goalkeeper and seven thousand people in the stadium went silent whilst three hundred others yet again dealt pandemonium.

Caspar lowered his forehead.

Athletic won the game 0 – 2. At the final whistle I spoke to Caspar,

"We still have to applaud the team at the end, boyo, even if we've lost."

I was sad when taking him down the stairs and he kept watching me, trying to read me. It was tragic that I'd taken to him to a shock loss as his debut game. And was keen to make up for it.

We got out to the bus stop again and it was blustery and cold and all these miserable fans poured beside us.

"It's all right, uncle," Caspar said to me, "it doesn't matter that we lost. Thanks for taking me anyway."

"Thank you too kiddo."

This was one of his finest quotes.

23

Kelsie got in touch with me just when it turned into November. She hadn't spoken to me since Tom and Miranda's funeral back in the summer. Nor had I thought about her much since then.

She was meek and polite on the phone. I wondered why I was calling and then the reason came up. She knew that Caspar's birthday was next weekend and she wanted to invite him over for a party at her and Mark's place with their kids.

"He used to come over almost every year in November," Kelsie explained, "and he loved it. Caspar gets on well with my kids too and they'd like to see him again."

"Yeah. Nice idea. What day are you thinking of?"

The day after his literal birthday she suggested which worked well cos I'd planned some more things with him on the specific day.

"Yes I'm sure he will enjoy it. I'll drive him up then."

"Okay good. How has Caspar been anyway since it all went down?"

"He's a buoyant lad. He's signed up to a football team and is playing for them each week. In school his grades are all good. Yeah, Caspar's an exceptional boy. I can see he'll be grand in life. I wouldn't have resurged like he's doing when I was that young."

She didn't seem charmed by these words. There was a trifle of small talk. And then she hesitated and paused. An eerie blip in the dialogue, nervous about saying something.

"Is something else on your mind Kelsie?"

"Just one thing."

"Tell me. Go for it."

"Do you want to come to Caspar's party as well? Here, I mean."

"Why would I … Do you mean you'd rather it was Caspar and yourselves at the party without me there?"

"No no no."

"I understand if you don't want me there."

"It's not that exactly. I may as well say it. If you do come can you please not drink?"

"I wasn't even thinking about alcohol Kelsie. If I'm driving the boy to and from the city then I couldn't drink anyway."

"Well what I meant about the party was that it would be a sleepover as well. Caspar can sleep over here and I can drive him back the next day. I should have said that from the start, sorry."

"Ah, right."

"Apologies, Ralph, I don't mean to insult you."

"I get it. Aye. Caspar will stay over at yours. It'll be a swell holiday for him. No problem. I don't mind driving him back the next day if it's easier?"

"No I can do that."

"Cool. Well, I shall tell Caspar the news I'm sure he'll be thrilled."

"Thanks, Ralph."

"Anything else for now?"

"I think that's it for now yeah."

"Night night then."

November came with its navy blue afternoon skies and heavy rain and wind. When I was a boy it would snow a lot during this month; nowadays it just rained, relentlessly.

I drove Caspar over to Kelsie's place for his party on the agreed date. He was buzzing about it. We got to Kelsie's lush house quite early (I didn't mean to get there so soon). And as we got into the driveway I saw Mark in the front garden. I waved to him uneasily. He didn't wave back so initially I thought that he didn't recognise my car because we hadn't neared the driveway yet. Then Mark went into his house. So I assumed that he hadn't seen us at all and then I drove into the driveway.

At the same moment, Kelsie and her kids came out, all smiling and fluttery.

Caspar run up to his friends/cousins and hugged them. Kelsie gave me this very brittle embrace and asked how the drive up was. Then Mark came out of the house again.

(He was a big man with prominent eyebrows and a wide jaw. An attractive guy to both sexes. Healthy, too; a thoroughly sober man, and, by the state of his house alone, wealthy, admirable, enviable.)

"Hey there Casp, little chum. I'm so glad to see you again," he said to my kid and then he bent down and cuddled him.

I went up to Mark. After he'd stood up.

"How you doing, Mark?" and I held out a palm for him to shake.

Mark didn't look at me. He turned back to the kids. They were fondling each other, playful as dogs.

"Come on into the house kids, let's get some juice and snacks." They yelled yay and then he walked on in after them. And shut the door.

The children didn't see what happened. Kelsie was the only one that did.

So now it was just her and I in the front of the house. She stayed outside with me.

"Can I speak to you for five minutes, Ralph?"

"Uh hu."

Kelsie and Mark both had these super posh cars which were way posher than mine and I wasn't threatened by them; I'd never understood why people feel it important to own a flashy automobile.

She led the way down to my modest/cheap car where she wanted to 'have a talk'.

"My husband ignored your handshake," she said.

"He did, yes. Why?"

"Is that a serious question?"

"Because of how I acted at the funeral?"

"What else would it be about?"

"What does it have to do with Mark? What's it got to do with him?"

"Do you realise how much of a bastard you can be, Ralph?"

I swallowed and my arrogance dissolved.

"Often I don't mean it," I said, "it pops out and it's not intended."

"Are you not ashamed about what you said about your brother at his funeral?"

"I am."

"So why can't you say sorry about it?"

"Sorry. I didn't know why I did that. It came out that way and I improvised and it was out of place."

"Were you drunk that day?"

"No, I wasn't."

"That's even more telling, then."

Kelsie was shivering with rage.

"Listen, I'm so sorry, Kelsie."

"You did that at my sister's send-off as well. I think about Miranda every day. You shamed her as well."

"This wasn't my intention. I didn't even know

Miranda so well."

Then Kelsie did something which I didn't expect. She took out a packet of cigarettes and slipped one of them out and lit one of them. I didn't know she smoked; she seemed like the kind of person who didn't. She offered me one but I declined.

"And what about me?" she continued, after a few puffs. "Have you never thought you could call to see how I'm doing? It's been – what – four months since my sister and your brother died. I'm grieving as well. I know me and you have never been close. But do you not think you can reach out to me? That we can talk about it."

"I was just concentrating on Caspar is all. I'm trying really hard with him."

"Good. That's good. But, are you not grieving for your brother?"

"It takes me a long time to approach things. I tend to block things off. It's just how I am."

"Even being sad about Tom?"

"Well, yes."

"Have you even cried about him since he passed?"

I realised that I hadn't and then as an answer I shook my head and Kelsie frowned.

"Apologies for being a grim presence at your party for Caspar, Kelsie. I'll let you go in and have fun now."

And I made to go back to my car.

"Ralph?" she called. I turned. She came up right in my face. "My husband, your brother – he loved you a lot. He just didn't know how to show it."

"I know."

"Did you ever show it to him?"

"I don't know."

We hugged each other and I got in my car and I

rolled the window down. Kelsie had a thin nose and she'd worn lipstick this morning and a skirt and she hadn't brought a coat out and this was part of the reason she shuddered.

"Ralph. If you bottle your horrible thoughts up all your life it will only end badly. You shouldn't think of yourself as the only troubled person ... everybody has issues. Please. Just call me if you're feeling low. I'd like to speak to you too on the phone if you want to? It would help me with Miranda. Tom as well."

"Thanks Kelsie. I will do."

"I'm not sure I believe you?"

"Have some faith, my friend. I want you to go and enjoy your party now, okay? Caspar's very fond of you. Thanks again."

I took off from the driveway. She waved me goodbye. The November streets were crisp and sunny in pink, blue and yellow and I was glad that the scene was over and that I was in a new film.

PART THREE

24

Let's bring the timeline of this book forward nine and a half years.

My nephew Caspar was sixteen and I was in my fifties. We stayed together in my new house which I'd taken a mortgage out on a few years back. The season was spring.

I was walking home from work. I'd finished a bit earlier than usual and it was late afternoon. Up ahead on the street I saw Caspar. He was walking the same way with his back to me and didn't know I was there. I would've called to him to get his attention. But he was with somebody. A girl.

I couldn't see her face but she had nice blonde hair. So I stopped going to fast and watched them. At the end of this street was a right turn onto the road where my house was. Caspar and the girl stopped there. They hugged. And then he kissed her on the lips. She went left and he went right. It was quite a charming sparkly moment; I'd never even heard Caspar talk about girls before.

For a while I waited on my road so I could give Caspar time to get inside. Then I went home. When I got in he'd already gone upstairs. He usually napped for an hour when he arrived back from school. I went in to the kitchen and made something to eat.

Caspar used to dine with me when he was smaller but he didn't do that these days. He wasn't interested in eating a meal with me – and in fact he ate very little, which was a bit concerning. So what I did was still make food for both of us and then I would leave a plate for him in the fridge. Which I did today.

Then I sat in the living room and read some of my book. It was this silly spy thriller but I was liking it. Some time later, Caspar came down stairs, puffy from his nap.

"Hey there Caspar," I said, "how was school?"

"Hey Ralph. It was shit."

"Ach well. There's some dinner in the fridge if you want."

"Thanks."

He did go into the fridge but he didn't take his plate out; he picked up the orange juice carton and drank from it at the window. I turned the corner in my book and went into the kitchen.

"So, ehh, Caspar?"

"Yeah?"

"I saw you earlier. Wasn't stalking you or anything. Umm. You were with a girl? Who was that?"

He had been looking at me and then his eyes shut down when I said this. He blushed. And I couldn't stop smiling.

"That your girlfriend, Casp?"

"Where did you ... Urgh."

"Haha. You should have told me you had a girlfriend."

He was still very red but he was smiling a little bit as well.

"I knew you'd get one eventually. Handsome chap like you. What's her name?"

"Oh, hush your face, Ralph. You're the creep who was spying on us."

He grinned when he put the juice back in the fridge.

"Come on, boyo, what's her name?"

"Carly."

"Nice name indeed. Nice that you have a girl too. How long you been dating?"

"Few months."

"You kept that hidden well! You don't have to be so secretive."

"Shoosh your mouth. Anyway, I'm gonna head up stairs. Thanks for the food I shall have some a bit later on."

He moved passed me. It was super rare to see Ralph embarrassed and even harder to tease him about things.

"Any plans for tonight, Casp?" I called as he was just about to go.

"Yeah actually I might head to the cinema later."

"Ooh, with Carly? How romantic."

He chuckled, and left.

I jogged through my thriller book downstairs. Later on I heard Caspar showering up stairs and then he came down stairs. He'd dressed smart and wore aftershave. Caspar had only recently started shaving and most of it grew in the moustache area (what in my part of the world we call 'bumfluff' – ha).

"You look good, sonny," I said to him, having gone to meet him in the hall.

"Ta."

"Have a nice time."

"Will do."

He moved towards the front door into the darker part of the hallway.

"Listen, Caspar, just one thing before you go. There's something I was wanting to ask you about. I just didn't get the chance yet."

"Okay?"

"K. Coach Munro called me the other day. He was concerned. Munro said you didn't turn up to training last week."

"Oh."

"How come you couldn't make training?"

"Coach called you personally?"

"Yeah. He was just worried is all."

"Ah. Well I made up for it at the weekend. I was back there for the Sunday session."

"Sure. But I just wondered why you weren't there last week."

"Oh. Well, it's a tad cringeworthy. I had diarrhoea that day, Ralph. Had the shits all day and it kinda put me off the training. Didn't want to shit myself on the pitch."

"Ah I see. Fine. But did you call up Munro to tell him that before the session?"

"I didn't, no. Was just too cringey to tell the reason."

"It's not that cringey. Caspar – if you're ill again and can't make it you need to call him up beforehand. So he's not wondering where you are. Okay?"

"I will do, uncle."

"Okay, thanks for being honest with me."

"No problem. Sorry about that blip. It won't happen again."

"Don't be. Anyway – what film you going to see?"

Caspar told me it was some superhero movie. One of those flashy modern ones which seem to have overtaken the blockbuster genre. Glitz and CGI and supernatural skills.

"Wow, that sounds really bad," I said.

"Yeah, I know. It was her choice. Not mine."

I sniggered. We said bye and he went.

I went into the kitchen and opened a beer and got

back to the novel and sat and read it and drank, thinking that there wasn't anything up with Caspar.

25

It was a strange thing to be in my fifties and witness my physical power waver.

Even after my football career ended I always made the effort to stay fit. Mostly with walking – an exercise which didn't exacerbate the kneecap injury so much. But now that I was older I couldn't walk so long without the cap getting sore all over again. So it tired me out and then I couldn't be as active.

There was a moment just recently (from this point in the narrative) when I was heading into town. My bus sailed down ahead of me. And I ran to catch it instinctively. My kneecap suddenly snapped and I had to stop and lean on a lamppost for five minutes. Thought I'd broken it again. (But I hadn't.)

Most people at some point in their lives which they owned a time machine, right?

If you could used the machine once and go back and make one change. Then face the consequences from there. Well, for me it would be avoiding that foul from that thug. It I'd just moved my leg half a yard in the other direction it wouldn't still hurt today. But nobody had concocted that most magical of machines just yet.

What I did have was a pleasant house and a decent income and a nephew, whom I'd managed to raise for nine and a half years on my own.

Caspar was now playing football for a professional club. Quite a good one too: they were called Albion. In the youth team obviously but he was still signed up. I tried to be as supportive as I could with that. And was proud.

In school he was a B slash C student. He seemed to be liked by lots of people. And my biggest hope for him for that he'd become a senior player one day. If he kept trying for the next two years he could be there. Start his career.

I hoped that he liked me as well. I wasn't sure if he did, in a conventional sense: especially the last few years. Things like him not wanting to eat with me, examples like that, were hurtful. But I mean I remembered being a teenager too and I could be a mean brat as well. Far more than he was. So my tactics were to be patient.

People were pleasant with me at work. That's where I got a section of my social interaction from. I never hung out with them outside of the workplace; I'd get invitations to staff parties and so on but always declined so they just stopped inviting me. Caspar, therefore, was my only significant other. And I was determined to make him somebody. He could reach adulthood and then leave me, go on his own path. If he wanted to stay in touch and seek me out for advice after that, then I was here; if not, then this was acceptable as well.

26

You know that first time I saw Caspar with Carly in the street? There was another weird moment relating to this which happened a week after that one did.

Once again, I had finished work early and went home in the late afternoon. It was hail-stoning heavily and I was running into the house to get out of the rushing street, though I enjoyed the storm.

The stones had gotten into my coat pockets and I stood inside the doorway tipping the mini white marbles onto the carpet and I took my shoes off. I knew that Caspar was already home because the lights were on and the door wasn't locked. The lights were on in the living room. So I called out to him.

"Woah that's come crazy hail," and I went into the living room.

And sitting on the sofa was not Caspar but this incredibly beautiful blonde girl who blinked up at me. The yellow hair clashed with her big eyes which were clad in black liner.

"Hello," I said.

There had never been a female in this house before and it was baffling. (There must've been when the previous occupants owned the building but as far as I could recall it was only me and Caspar, almost exclusively. There'd been a boiler guy once. A joiner. When the boiler decided to go bust one winter. But that was it.)

The girl didn't say hello back. I bowed down to her and offered a handshake: it was all I could think of.

"I'm Ralph, nice to meet you."

"Nice to meet you."

Her wrist was so small I could've cracked it.

"What's your name?"

"Carly."

She really was exotic looking and I felt glad for Caspar.

Then there was a flush of the toilet down the hall. And Caspar came out of the toilet, beginning a new sentence. He didn't know I was in the house; hadn't heard me come in: and was calling out to Carly, thinking she was the only one in the room and then he came in to the doorway and see me and he froze with fear and stared at me.

"Hey there champ," I said. "I got away from work early."

Caspar was so humiliated he looked ill. I felt bad that he was so bashful and Carly was looking up at him and they'd both gone silent.

"I'm just gonna go make some coffee. Would you chaps like anything?"

"No, thank you," Carly said.

Caspar shook his head. I'd actually planned to start making some food in the kitchen rather than just coffee. But now that I'd spoiled the mood in the other room I just did the coffee and went back there with my steaming mug. Caspar hovered in the centre of the room. Carly on the couch.

"Well, I'll see you chaps later on," I said. "I'm just gonna go upstairs and read. You guys doing anything tonight?"

"Yes we'd thought we'd go and hang out with the chums at the park."

"Sounds cool. See you later on tonight."

They mumbled a farewell.

Both of them exited the house quickly after this scene. And Caspar was gone for four hours. Following which, he came into the house again. (I'd made him some food earlier and had eaten and was upstairs in my bedroom, nearing the end of thriller novel ((the spy was in some intensely toxic situation which he needed to escape from)).)

I heard Caspar come up the stairs. And had expected to hear his light switch click in the next room. But instead there was a knock on my door.

"Come in?"

He appeared.

"Hey there Ralph."

"Caspar, my friend, what's up?"

"I just wanted to come say something."

"All right. Shoot."

"I'm sorry for what happened earlier."

"What happened earlier?"

"You know. The thing with … her."

"What was bad about it?"

"I should have asked you if she could come in to the house first."

"Not at all, lad."

"I know you were pissed off about it."

"I wasn't angry at all, Casp. You've got it all wrong."

"Oh. I just thought you were annoyed?"

"No. Not one bit."

"Cos you don't like people in the house, is all."

"Nah. Nah – it's only because I have no friends who come to visit me. Ho ho. You can bring friends over whenever you like."

"I can?"

"Of course."

"Okay, thanks. I think I misunderstood then."

"Yeah but that's cool as well."

"I'll say good night for now then."

"Night night Caspar. Be well."

I still think about this conversation with him a lot. And do not fully understand why he felt he had to come and say this to me, as if he knew I was angry, when I wasn't. It made me a tyrant when I wasn't trying to be.

27

There's one other thing I should mention. This thing I kept doing during this period. I've never spoken about it to anybody and so I suppose it's a type of confession. And you might find me wacky for admitting it. But here it goes.

I developed a habit of driving up to see my father's grave. He was retired on a lonely graveyard in the north of the city – one of those yards which had long been filled up and that nobody visited. It was perched on a hillside and you could see out for far spans across the town. I didn't bring flowers to his tombstone. He wouldn't have appreciated that; he wasn't that kind of man. What I would do was just sit there on the bench which was handily nearby.

And speak to him. I'd say, "Hey there Pop." And there was a tingly vibe to knowing that he was so nearby.

In the past I would go and do that on his birthday and would simply sit with him for a period. Annually I would go and visit him on the day he was born. (And that was already some lengthy time too, almost ninety years back.) But then there was one of his birthdays it was a particularly merry morning. And I said, "Good morning, Pop." And sat.

And then I just kept speaking to him. Even though he couldn't answer. The cemetery was deserted. I didn't have to speak up. And the graveyard being at such a height, the wind muffled my words. But it did seem like he was listening. My old man.

It did occur to me that I was going crazy. So I stopped and I went home.

That same night, I had a dream about my father. I was a kid again and he was in the garden and we worked on a new project that needed fixing. The dream isn't worth retelling. Had no action in it. But the main point is that he was alive and speaking to me again in his curt way. Dad could do the random joke. I laughed in the dream. And laughed in real life and then I woke up and I was only fifty-something Ralph Ballard again.

So very soon after that I went back to his tomb and spoke to him in a similar way.

I told him about Caspar and wondered what he thought about how I'd done with raising him? (My father had only met Caspar when he was a baby. It was right before he died, actually.) I asked him what the afterlife was like. Did he think I'd failed as an athlete? That I could have done better as a younger man if my attitude had improved – if I had taken care of the health better and not drank so much.

In this way, I was confessing to him. Things which I had wanted to say to him decades ago when I had the chance. But I hadn't the courage.

That same night after I'd gone home I dreamed about him again. It was a nondescript, plotless dream but he had resurfaced again. He was in the living room in the old house and he was working on something in the kitchen with bangs and pops and he called me to come give him a hand.

It was my way of making him alive again.

The irony was that he did speak to me in the dreams. But it wasn't related to any of the questions that I tried in front of his gravestone. And when I woke up I couldn't remember the dialogue exactly.

Do you think this was a bizarre thing to do? I'm guessing yes. It was my way of therapy, in a sense. Speaking to myself in a cemetery was the manner in which I could try and process what bothered me.

I did this for quite some time. And it worked well for my mental health. When Caspar was unaware or when I had some free time I would head to the graveyard.

It got complicated when my father stopped making cameos in my dreams.

He didn't turn up when I slept anymore, and this affected my sleeping. Because it had made me look forward to sleep – knowing he would make a cameo. Then he didn't, even though I'd been to the yard earlier that day. And I would lie awake. Try to force myself to dream. This didn't occur and then I would be moody and irritable during work in the daytime because I hadn't rested.

Throughout that winter I spoke to my father's tomb more and more in the hope that he would come back to me when I slept. It got pretty deranged. I'd talk to him out loud – and I'd sit in front of the tombstone rather than on the bench – for an hour straight.

"Please come and see me tonight, Pop," I pleaded.

Yes, I was deteriorating. My sanity was moving different places.

And then there was one occasion where I was speaking to my father again, in a feverish, manic way.

I heard a noise behind me and I turned. And there was this woman walking towards me. The noise came from her little dog, which had barked. I sat up. The woman stared at me and she was hesitant to come on down the path and the waif dog was wary of me too.

That moment shocked me. What was I doing to myself? I turned away from father and walked the other way and out of the cemetery.

When the spring emerged I did want to go back to the grave again. But I had the sensation that I might get caught out again. That I was doing something criminal rather than therapeutic with it.

The spring plants popped up with their raw colours and Caspar was now doing different things with his life and I had a lot of chances to go and see my father again, but I dallied and shut that option off. It was easier to trap stuff away. Be a normal man. Nullify it with alcohol. Be what I was supposed to be. A nobody.

Not only did my dreams not involve my Dad: they slipped away altogether. I didn't dream about anything. I'd sleep and would black out and would wake up and head to the office and that was it.

28

Caspar spent more and more time out of the house. I presumed with his lass. It was fine. I got it. He was young and experiencing a new form of love with a girl. It was innocent.

But he was also barely communicating with me. I didn't see him. And he'd come back late on the week nights. Late enough to wake me up when I'd retired upstairs. March turned to April and it was an especially warm one. There was a bank holiday when Caspar stayed away for days at friend's houses and probably his girlfriend's. (I'd only met her that one time in the house and hadn't seen her again.) And there was no word from him whatsoever.

The days outside were glorious with sun and scent and hue. I understood that he was having fun. I just wished that Caspar would respond to my text messages, asking where he was.

There were other concerns too.

In the late nights or early mornings when he finally returned home I smelled alcohol and marijuana off of him. It stank on his clothes and lingered in the hallway. And I understood all that too. I smoked a lot when I was a teen. Was standard adolescent behaviour.

But he wouldn't be able to smoke if he wanted to be a proper soccer player cos it would turn up in his piss tests. It would also destroy his motivation and make him stupid.

As for alcohol ...

Well, as you already know. I had/have my own problems with that. So I didn't know how to confront him seriously about it. Approach him, rather. Because he knew that I still drank too much as well. I couldn't tell him not to indulge with that worst of drugs. If I did so myself.

I was worried, and stuck, about Caspar. Perhaps it was a phase with him that would eventually pass? I hoped.

At the same time, I noticed that he was pilfering my beers from the fridge in the kitchen too. Due to the length of my addiction, I knew how many cans/bottles I had at home. Kept tabs on what I had. Caspar didn't know I knew he was stealing them. It wasn't that many – only one or two now and then but I was still aware. I didn't want to get aggressive with him about it. I wasn't his father. Only an uncle. So what I did was keep my own alcohol in my room so he couldn't get at it. And had to rely on warm beer from then on. (Poor me.)

As I say, I was still sanguine that these were all temporary worries.

29

I got a phone call from Coach Munro one morning. My nephew's manager. Head of the Albion youth team.

Munro was a gruff, shrewd, older gentleman who had been in the game for decades. Like me, he used to play professionally and he had managed many clubs after that and he was old now, close to retirement. I liked him. He was scary – in a good way – he certainly intimidated me whenever I encountered him.

And so I got nervous when I saw who was calling. Sat up from the sofa and prepared for it. I was home alone. Caspar was off out with his cronies again.

"Hello?"

"Hi there, Ralph. How are you doing?"

"I'm good thanks. Yourself?"

"Not too shabby. Do you have a spare five minutes for us to talk?"

"Sure, I'm all free."

"As you've probably guessed, it's about your nephew."

"Right. Ah. What's happened? Did he miss training again?"

"Yes, actually. He's missed a few meetings since I last spoke to you. He'll call me up in the daytime and say he can't come, for whichever reason. I'd hoped it would be only a handful of times. But I've seen this type of behaviour in young men before. And I know that he's lying."

"I'll speak to him, Coach. I'll straighten him out. Jesus – I told him not to –"

"Ralph. Just hear me out. There's more to it than the training thing. Because he does still attend most of the sessions. It's about his overall game."

"Okay?"

"You come to his matches, right?"

"I do."

"So you've noticed he's not been playing nearly as well as he used to."

"Yes, I have noticed that."

"If it were Christmas time last year he'd immediately be in my first team. Now we're in April and I think of him more as a substitute. He hasn't scored since January, and he used to be one of my most promising forwards."

"I've been thinking about this as well. I think his self esteem has taken a bruising of late."

"Why is that?"

"Well, for one thing, I know he hates being put on the bench from the start."

"We all do. It's not that simple. Why has his confidence plummeted this year?"

"I do not know why. I'm not as close to my nephew as I used to be, and he's quite hard to get through to. He's kinda in those difficult teenage years, you know …"

"I'm not trying to be offensive, or trying to overstep my boundaries here, Ralph."

"Of course, Coach."

"Has anything happened in his personal life this year which has hurt him?"

I thought about mentioning the alcohol and marijuana thing. But, Munro was a huge disciplinarian. When I first got the phonecall I thought this was the reason for the reach-out. If I told Munro about that it would be me snitching Caspar out. Couldn't do that.

Then I thought about telling him about the girlfriend thing. But this seemed so silly that it couldn't be relevant.

"Coach, I can't think of any fundamental thing with him that's gone wrong. But, I'll speak to him."

"Please do. Because you know I do believe there's a great player in there. But if he keeps playing like this then I won't be able to keep him on. The summer break will be in two months. He needs to improve by then."

"It's as serious as that, Coach? You're thinking about releasing him?"

"Well, I'll be straight with you, Ralph. Yes. He needs to be more focused and return to the standards I know he's capable of."

"Oh. I'm all worried now too."

"I felt I had to speak to you, Ralph."

"I know. Thank you."

"But I haven't told you yet about the main reason I'm calling. It's not just about his form and attitude. There's something a bit different."

"Please tell me."

"In the changing rooms at the last game. At the end of the match. We'd lost. As you know. And Caspar had only played ten minutes at the end and he'd barely gotten a touch of the ball. The lads were getting changed out of their strips. Most of them had gone home. I was about to go home too. Then I realised I'd forgotten my water bottle.

"So I went back in to the rooms to get it. And Caspar was the last boy in there. He had his strip off. And so I could see his naked chest. I noticed there were marks on them. Cuts."

A hard wave of sadness went through me and I dropped my forehead.

"Did you know about this, Ralph?"

"No, I didn't."

"…"

"So it looked like self harm?"

"I only saw it for a second. He didn't know I was there and flinched when he saw me and turned around. And I didn't say anything to him either; I just said bye and he did as well. But yes it certainly looked as if he was harming himself."

"Thanks for telling me this news, Coach."

This sentence was so ironic and I only realised after saying it. My voice fluttered too.

"Your nephew is a fantastic football player, Ralph. He's obviously got some mental problems that need addressing. I wouldn't want to see him wasted. And I believe that he can come back to us and stay with the team. Do you agree?"

"I totally agree."

"And let me know if I can help in any way. I can speak to him too, if you like. I just wanted to let you know first because you're his guardian."

"Definitely. You're a fair man, Coach."

"I'll say good evening for just now. Do keep in touch."

"I shall."

30

That same night I thought about driving up to see Dad again to ask his advice on what to do about Caspar.

But I didn't think I could be within the vicinity of my father's skeleton. I was too ashamed to be near him. I was the one who was alive and still had my body and it was me who had to act, to use his own compass.

My resolution was to demand that Caspar speak to me one on one. I would force him into a dialogue as soon as he got home that evening. Had had enough. And was sick with fretting about him.

He still wasn't home by midnight. I'd already texted him earlier in the evening,

'When will you be home, Casp?'

And he texted back about one o'clock,

'I'll be home tomorrow, uncle. x'

It was a relief to get a reply from him for once. And frankly, I was so tried out from stress that I wasn't in fit shape to speak to him so late.

In my house I had a little office where I kept my books and most precious things. Amongst the precious items was a photograph of my father.

It was in black & white. And the photograph itself was, wow, around seventy years old. I'd framed it a long time ago. Because it was such a brilliant photo of him. He was grinning because he was camera shy. My mother had taken the pic – when they weren't married yet and hadn't had Tom or I. He was young and his teeth shone out in ivory.

I didn't say anything to the photo.

It was just that I couldn't sleep for hours … stayed up until four in the morning. And thought it might help to see Dad. It did. I smiled. And got back to sleep after that.

31

Caspar did come home, the next evening. I'd been preparing what to say to him all day.

I met him when he came in. He waved and smiled when he saw me but his face was lethargic.

"Evening, Ralphie," he said.

"Hello Casp. What you been up to?"

"Ah, just mooching about."

I got the funk of alcohol off of him and he was avoiding eye contact.

"I'm just gonna go up stairs and take a shower."

"Okay. Hey there, chum: is it okay if I spoke to you one on one for a bit after your shower?"

"What about?"

"Ah. Nothing to worry about – just a few things. That okay?"

"Can it wait until tomorrow? I'm quite tired. I was planning to head to sleep after the shower."

"Just if we could speak tonight, that would be much appreciated."

"Okay."

He took a long time in the shower. Then he spent a long time in his room. Was he dodging me? I waited 40 minutes for him to give any sign he was supposed to come and talk, and I was about to call him from downstairs but didn't want to nag. Then he arrived by his own volition.

And suddenly he was in the living room with me and I realised this was the first one on one 'chat' I'd had with my nephew and this said a lot about me as an uncle and I wasn't sure how to go about it.

"So how's it going, Caspar?"

"Not bad. What do you want to talk about?"

"I suppose … the main thing is that I feel you've

gone away from me a wee bit this year."

"Really? I thought we were close. We're mates, aren't we?"

"Of course we're mates. That's not what I mean. I feel there's something you're not telling me."

"Like what?"

"As a start … umm, have you been drinking tonight?"

"Have *you*?"

"No, not tonight."

"Well that's unusual."

"There's no need to be mean. I was only wondering."

"I had some beers at Justin's house."

"Alcohol will affect your football. Is the only thing I'm suggesting."

"Well yeah, it will."

"How are you feeling about your sport, my nephew? These days."

"Ralph. Did Coach Munro call you again?"

"Yes, he did."

"I knew it! He can be a bit of a rat, can't he."

"No. He's not a rat. Don't use that word about that Coach."

"…"

"He did call me yeah but I've been wishing to speak with you for some time. It's hard for me to … express. And connect."

"Because of your Asperger's thing?"

"How'd you know about the Asperger's?"

"Mum mentioned it to me when I was a kid. She said you were an Aspie. And I didn't know what it meant for years. Until I looked it up. Online – it told me all of the traits. And it made more sense to me after I did that."

"How's that? What are you meaning?"

"Just cos of the way you are. Your mannerisms."

"Okay."

"What's the point in speaking to an Aspie?"

"Why do you say these hurtful things, Caspar? I'm still your uncle. Not your enemy."

His expression was difficult to pinpoint throughout the dialogue. It was as if he wasn't my nephew, not anybody. He opened his mouth to say something. But never did. So I continued.

"Let's get back to the original point. Your sport. Please tell me how you feel about it?"

"What's 'my sport'?"

"Do you want to be an Albion player or not?"

"You've never even asked me about this before."

"I thought you wanted to succeed as a footballer?"

"Well ... I thought I was in to it when I was younger. But I'm not so positive anymore."

"Why? Not keen on the game?"

"Uncle. It's fairly simple. I don't think I'm that talented."

"You are! You're a cracking player!"

"If you want an answer then that's what's been bothering me since last year."

"What makes you think you're not a good player?"

"I am *good*. But I'm not great, and never will be. If I haven't shown it so far. I'll be seventeen this year and I'll have to enter the next draft. Am I really worthy of the draft?"

"But this decline has only been less than half a year. You can bounce back."

"So you agree that I've been in decline – there you go."

"Your form has dipped. But this happens with many athletes. Sport is about overriding complication.

I'm just wondering why you're not interested in doing that?"

"Maybe I'm not."

He wasn't giving me the answers I wanted to hear. He was falling away from me. I held on to him but he wasn't trying to climb up.

"Is it something about your particular team?" I said. "Albion?"

"Yes. In a way."

"You don't get on with the boys?"

"No, not really. They're all idiots, Ralph. Morons. You know they are."

"Immature, maybe."

"Aye."

"They're promising athletes as well."

"Are they? I don't think I'll be watching them on the TV in a few years' time. I doubt it."

"You can be the best of them. Move on from Albion."

"I just don't believe in that concept of 'the best' anymore. If there is a number one best then I will never be that."

"This is not the mentality to have."

"Who's talking?"

"Me."

"From experience, I mean, who is talking to me about this?"

"… Well, me, Caspar."

"Why would I listen to a failed footballer?"

I looked at him dead on and he looked back at me dead on. He kept going.

"When you were sixteen you were already signed for Rovers, right? You were in their youth team. Rovers are better than Albion. Then you made it in to the Rovers first squad and you had a few successful years in your early twenties. The crowds loved you. You scored. You scored that famous goal against United which my Dad used to play me on video.

"Rovers didn't even win that game. Your goal was an equaliser, not a winner. Then you didn't score at all for the next two seasons. And the season after that, Rovers sold you to a smaller club. Your career perked up a bit and you were doing better. But you got a bad injury which forced you to quit. And I looked up a video to see the injury. The other bloke got sent off for it. I couldn't even find a video for it. That incident was famous for you but not other people.

"And that's it. That's all you were as a player. And I will never be as good as you. You were a better player than I am. And you're the failure. What would be the point in going on this huge adventure knowing that it would be a disaster in the end?

"I'm not a child anymore, uncle. It's stupid to believe in dreams which aren't realistic. I know that you wanted me to be a star and so on. But that won't happen."

He watched me for an answer. And it took me a while to emit a sentence. It felt like my whole body was depressed, that my tongue couldn't work either and that I could only breathe. Caspar had spoken without pause. He dallied over no line and he'd obviously *wanted* to say them to me; they'd been pent up inside him and he'd prepared their delivery.

"I thought football was our thing, something that we shared," I finally said, "that it was my way of being your uncle."

"Yeah I know. It used to be. I appreciate you taking me to games and supporting me."

"Can I tell you something?"

"Um hmm?"

"I agree with you in a few ways. I do know the sport more than you. And, yes, at the age of sixteen I was in a more illustrious position. But I've known many athletes from their earlier ages. And I always thought you were better than me. That's where we differ.

"In fact. When you were a boy and I saw you play, I almost didn't want to get you into the game because I felt threatened that you would overtake me. But I decided to help you with it for the same reason, from the opposite perspective. Because I wanted you to be a champion, more than I was."

"I don't feel the same way, uncle."

"So that's it? You're just going to give up with Albion?"

"I haven't made a final decision yet."

We sat for a long while in silence.

"I'm really tired, Ralph," he finally said. "Is it all right if I turn in for the evening?"

I needed to ask him about the scars. The self harm. But it seemed wrong to do it at this point. And the dialogue had already been so draining.

"Okay. But, Caspar?"

"Yeah?"

"Can we please talk about something else soon?"

"Sure."

"Nothing about football at all. Nothing about that. I need to talk to you about another thing, is that fine?"

"Yes. No worries. Another time."

I got up when he got up and I gave him a handshake. Then he went upstairs to his room.

32

The next day I went into work. The office environment and the workload in front of the computer were beneficial because it helped me take my mind off of things. Concentrate on other things. And then by the evening I was done.

And it was a pretty April evening. Cloudless and all those colours in the sky on the verge of twilight. Made me not want to go home just yet. Felt like doing something different. My office building was near the coast – was in this warehouse district on the other side of the city close to the harbour. Which meant lots of gulls and gritty wind.

I thought I'd go along to the esplanade and walk along it. Hadn't done that in a while.

The sea was this massive imposing span stretching in purple with these tiny orange oil ships being the only specks on the horizon and I imagined how far I could swim into the expanse before I drowned. The tide was out so I went onto the beach. It was scrawny and litter-clad. My shoes scrunched over the rocks and I went to the end of the water and picked up some pebbles and tried to do that skimming trick – is that what you call it? I tried like five times and the last one worked, bouncing on the waves and I cheered for myself.

Then I walked along the coast and climbed the stairs back onto the esplanade and then up the grassy sand dunes. There was a lil train through the sharp grass and along the way I found a kid's hat. This frilly thing. She (it was a girl's hat) must've dropped it and it was kinda hidden under the brush, so I picked it up and hooked it on a tree branch in case she came back to look for it, so she might find it more easily.

After the dunes there was the shape of the theme park in the distance and beyond that the mall complex. I'd never actually been to the theme park. In fact, I've never been on a rollercoaster in my life. Does this make me lame? I walked past the park and through the mall car park and I saw the sign of the cinema and I thought why not take a look at what's on? So I went into the complex and was met with tangy white light and echoes of feet and voices across the squeaky floor and I went into the atrium of the cinema.

80% of the list was stuff I had no interest in. But there was one film which had this actor in it which I liked. I bought a ticket and went in. Luckily there were few people in the theatre and I sat at the back.

So here's the film synopsis: the lead guy (the actor I admired) is this university lecturer who was very clever but a bit dislikeable and arrogant. He lives alone, works intensely in the day, and drinks at night. One day he's suddenly accused of plagiarism by the university and is suspended. Or rather, he's accused by some of his colleagues of plagiarism. From the start he screams his own innocence but he has to figure out a way to do that.

He has a history of intense anxiety and his anxiousness builds and builds until it ejaculates in these obscure panic attacks. And there's a great bit in the film where he has a fit in his local supermarket and nobody knows what's up with him because it's freaky. They call an ambulance for him but by the time the paramedics come he's fine again. So he runs away from the scene with everybody staring at him.

In order to combat the plagiarism thing he challenges the academic board. He comes up with evidence that the colleagues who accosted him were trying to frame him. It was them who fragmented the damning evidence in the first place and it had nothing to do with him. So it's him versus this elite of threatened academics who wanted to oust him for their own personal reasons.

And then the film kinda became a courtroom drama type deal and I suppose it was a bit gushing and silly at points and I didn't quite get all of the jargon. But, I liked it. Good movie.

Oh, and, the main character wins his case at the end and the baddies get caught out. And the university offer him the chance to go back to teaching/working. But he decides that he's fed up with academia and still feels betrayed that the institution suspended him. So he resigns and figures he'll do something else with his life.

I'd give it 4/5. I left the theatre and when I got outside I found a lot of the mall still open. The film hadn't been as long as I thought. So I moseyed about.

And I found one of those corporate bars down the hall. Chain bars, I mean. I couldn't remember the last time I'd actually drank in a bar. Since I was an isolated drinker. There weren't that many people inside, else I wouldn't have gone in.

I went up to get served and there was this older man behind the counter.

"Evening, sir, what can I get you?"

"A stout, please, sir."

He poured it expertly.

"Been up to much this evening?" he said.

"Yeah I just saw a movie upstairs."

"Oh yeah, which one was it?"

I told him the name of the film and the famous actor and asked him if he'd seen it.

"Ha. Nah – I'm not interested in that pretentious

shit. I'm sure it's a great film but that's not my cup of tea."

I chuckled.

"What's your name my friend?"

"Ralph."

"I'm Martin."

His fingers were solid.

"So what kind of movies are you in to then, Martin?"

"My favourite flick of all time is *Terminator 2: Judgement Day*. I don't care what anybody says, or if you judge me for it. The hell with it. I've seen that film 200 times and it never gets old."

"Haha yeah it's a classic, I agree."

And we got talking about James Cameron's other movies and I bought another stout. Martin was an easy going guy and I wished I had that natural manner like he had.

This all occurred on a Friday evening, by the way. So I said to Martin,

"You working this weekend as well?"

"No, my man! I've got the weekend off for once."

"Ah, great. Any plans for it?"

"Actually, I do. My daughter is getting married tomorrow."

"Woah, amazing. You must be chuffed."

"I am. Here, I'll show you a pic of her," and he took his phone out and showed me a photo of a normal looking girl smiling at the camera, "isn't she a beaut? The only thing is that I've got to make a speech tomorrow, cos I'm her Dad."

"Ha. How you feeling about that?"

"Terrified."

"I would be as well. How many people are going to the wedding?"

"Like two hundred."

"I feel for you Martin. But, it's good to be a little geared up on nerves as well."

"Ho. I've got the speech verbatim in my head."

"You'll nail it."

"What about you, Ralph, are you married?"

"Nah. No."

"Any kids?"

"Nope. I couldn't raise any children. Wouldn't be good at that. Don't have the skills."

"Ach, well – raising kids isn't all that fun, I can tell you. I feel my daughter owes me a celebration tomorrow after all the money I've put into her across her life."

"I hope it's an ace day. Glad for you."

33

When I got home that night I went to bed straight away. Throughout the morning I thought I heard movement downstairs. A few times. They weren't alarming noises or anything. There was definitely a point when the front door opened and closed, and this wasn't too unusual – for Caspar to come back late at night.

But then I heard it open and close again when I wasn't so fully asleep, and I looked at the clock and it was six in the morning. I was still needing a few more hours of wink and so I stayed in bed.

At about nine I got up and went downstairs. Was another pearly day outside the windows and I went into the kitchen to boil the kettle. There was a note left on the table. It was in Caspar's handwriting. And it said:

Dear Uncle,

I regret a lot of what I said the other night. It was overly mean, what I said, and I feel bad about it already. Sorry. I hope you can forgive. There's nothing concrete I've decided about my life just yet. I've gone different places this year and not all of them have been good. But this doesn't mean I can't improve. Anyway, sorry again, and I shall see you tomorrow or at the game on Monday. (I'm still in the squad for the Monday night game. I will probably be on the bench again but I will turn up to see if I get a game or not.) Caspar x

P.S. I'm staying out with mates today and won't be back tonight.

"Hmm," I said aloud. There was a mix of emotions when I read it. I don't think he'd ever written me a letter or note before. It was filled with mistakes whereby he'd had to bludgeon out words with the biro ink.

I made some coffee and read the letter again. There was an urgency to text him back quickly, and so I did so, and I said:

Thanks for your message in the kitchen, Casp. I just read it. Thank you for your apology as well – I accept that. Don't overthink it. And, yes, I'll see you at the Albion ground on Monday night. Or are you coming back here tomorrow evening to get ready? Ralph x

Was I sure whether I'd accepted his apology? I couldn't be … the memories of his lines were still fresh and I hadn't addressed them yet.

Caspar almost never replied on his phone on Saturdays and so I didn't expect to get one back from him today. And I went about doing relaxed stuff with my free time. He usually came back the evening before a game. To shower and get a decent night's sleep, etc. So I expected to see him on the Sunday.

34

But he didn't come home.

It got to the evening and then night. I had to speak to him about the self harm thing. And I blasted myself for not having had the gall to mention it to him before when he was here. That was my main intention – why hadn't I tried! Things like that are way more important than football. Jesus.

I'd already texted him in the evening to ask him if he was coming back. By night time I decided to call. It rang out. So I called again afterwards and it went to answerphone. And I left this message to him:

"Hey there, Caspar. Hope you had a good weekend. I thought you were coming back here tonight? If not, see you tomorrow. Anyway … umm. There was one thing I wanted to speak to you about when you were here last. It's … I don't know how to say it.

"When I was speaking to Coach Munro he mentioned something that was nothing to do with football. He wasn't ratting you out or anything. Munro noticed a thing on your body in the changing rooms. Marks? Were they cuts, Caspar? I don't mean to sound melodramatic and maybe Munro got it totally wrong. But I just wanted to check with you about that … Are they cuts?

"Because if they are then I understand all of that. I self harmed when I was young too. Please speak to me about that if that's the case. And please please please don't do it again if this is what it is. It gets worse if you try to hide it. Or if you try it again. Because you can go too far with it.

"If you don't wanna go to the game tomorrow and instead speak to me about this then that's cool. The

Coach will understand.

"Again, I could have let my imagination wander and if I've got this incorrect then sorry. Let me know. Okay ... bye bye for now then. Night night."

It was weird speaking to a space of air like that, within my silent house. And my voice got a bit squirmy and insecure. Wasn't sure whether I had done well.

The next day I was back in the office. And there were fewer workdays wherein I'd such a revulsion for this boring work and hated myself for having put myself in this dull situation. I really wanted to walk out. Throughout the hours, all of them were horrible, and it was perfectly possible to simply bail and never come back. Sack myself. But instead I stayed and tapped at the keys and stared at the spreadsheets.

The one good bit was that I tanked through the work and so I could go home earlier.

I got back into my district. The trees were all muggy in green and blossom and there were those effeminate scents of pollen from the gardens and I should've appreciated the spring weather.

Still no word from Caspar.

There was my house. I went to put the key in the front door. Turned it ... and found that it was already unlocked.

Went inside.

"Caspar?" I called. "Casp? Are you home?"

His shoes weren't in the hallway. He wasn't in the living room or kitchen. But there was a used glass on the table with pulpy bits of orange juice on it.

I went upstairs to his bedroom and his door was shut.

"Are you in there, Caspar?" knocking, "you sleeping?"

There was no answer so I opened the door and he wasn't inside. So I went to his window, which overlooked the garden, hoping he might have gone out there to sit on the grass. No.

I was panting now. And my pulse was manic. Plus, I really needed to piss; I went into the toilet and did that. Then washed my face and the salt from the length of the hot day went into my lips. I then went into my room and took my work shoes off.

And called Caspar to find out where he was now and why he'd left the house unlocked. Selected his name and tapped the green button.

This melodic singing came from out in the hall and it made me jump. I followed the noise, back into Caspar's bedroom.

His phone was left on his bedside table, flashing, ringing and buzzing with these gnarly raps.

Stupid me:

His phone rang out when I stood there blinking at it. Then I foolishly hung up when it went to answerphone. And his screen went blank. It would have been better to look through his phone to see who he'd been in contact with. But then it locked after I ended the call ... and I didn't know his pin to get back into it.

I thought that he had just been clumsy today. With the front door, and he'd forgotten to take his phone with him. When he went to the Albion ground to gear up before the game.

I sought around the house to check for further clues, as to anything he'd left behind or whatnot.

Nothing.

He must have gone down to check in with the team and I should go there now. Drive down. It's close. I took his phone and put it in my pocket. Then I got changed into civilian clothes and I drank a pint of water downstairs – my face was dripping and hair greasy.

Locked the front door and drove down to the Albion ground. The youth team played in a smaller stadium that only had small terraces; it used to be the main/adult team stadium location one hundred years back, which made it kind of romantic. But yeah, it housed about 4000 people, if that. The capacity I mean. I liked going there. Was a charming lil place.

I drove into the carpark around the back. There was a smaller building behind the stadium (wherein the players got changed and the staff had their offices) wherein I knew where to find the team.

Bear in mind that this was still three hours before the game was supposed to begin: there were few people about in the building. But I said Hi to the receptionist girl who I knew already.

"Hi there Cassie."

"Hi, Ralph."

"Is Coach Munro in yet?"

"Yeah he's in his office."

"Brilliant, thanks."

Through airy corridors I walked too fast and then I was at Munro's door which was already open and I peered inside and the white-haired, rather short, clean, respectable man was at his desk looking over paperwork. I knocked. He looked up.

"Mr Munro," I said.

"Ralph?" he put his pen down and leaned back. "What are you doing here?"

"I was looking for … I just came in to see you."

"Grand. Come in and take a seat."

"So what's brought you here so early, Ralph?"

"Caspar. I thought he might be here."

"No. He's not here. None of the boys are here yet. But they should get in around six o'clock or so."

"Great. So Caspar will be here at six o'clock?"

"Well, no."

"Why!"

"Didn't he tell you as well?"

"Tell me what?"

"He called me earlier. Said he was ill. That he can't play tonight."

"…"

Munro frowned and he stood up from his desk. He sat on the corner of the desk nearby me and looked down at me and imposed me with that scary face of his.

"Caspar called me and did one of his excuses again. He's done that before, as you know, with training, and far too many times. But he's never done it with a match before. What's up with your nephew, Ralph? He's obviously got some problems. What's the dilemma here?"

"When did he call you?"

"It was in the morning. I think about ten. So you haven't spoken to him today at all?"

"No. Haven't heard from him in days. How did he sound on the phone?"

"Well. He did sound like he was ill. But it was just another lie. He said he had an upset stomach but I could tell it was another sickie. He's just deciding not to come in."

"Ok. Thanks for your time, Munro. As always."

I stood up to leave. Was keen to get out of there.

"What do you think has happened with Caspar?" he said.

"I'm not sure Coach. Not right now, but I need to know."

I gave him a handshake.

"Ralph," he called, as I was leaving the office, "just wait a minute."

"Cheers, Coach. I have to get going with other things."

35

I got back into my car. And looked through my contacts on my phone. To try and find somebody else who might know where Caspar was.

Caspar had this best mate called Justin. And I had his number. Justin was a nice kid and I think Caspar had given me his number ages ago when he was younger, when he first started 'sleepovers' at his place.

I assumed that was where he'd gone on Saturday. Never in my life had I spoken to this boy via telephone. It felt like a creep calling up this other sixteen year old boy.

Justin picked up fast.

"Hi?"

"Hi there Justin it's Caspar's uncle."

"Okay ..."

"Ralph."

"Yeah, what's up?"

"Just wondered if Caspar is with you?"

"Ehh. No."

"He's not?"

"Nah."

"Well have you seen him today?"

"No."

"Were you with him at the weekend?"

"Last time I saw him was Saturday."

"At what time?"

"Oh it was really early. He went home from mine, maybe, two o'clock."

"In the afternoon?"

"No, morning. Is something wrong?"

"Yes! Something's wrong – I think Caspar's in danger. And would you please sharpen up a bit and help me out with this? Don't you care about your friend!"

"Sorry."

"What about his girlfriend?"

"You mean Carly?"

"Yeah."

"She's not his girlfriend anymore."

"Oh."

"Uh hu."

"When did that happen? The break-up I mean."

"Last week … Caspar told me."

"Did she break it off with him?"

"Yeah I think so."

"You think so or you know so?"

"She ended it, yes."

"Well how did Caspar take it – was he hurt?"

"He was upset yeah. But I didn't know how to talk to him about it."

"What did he say?"

"He just mentioned it …"

"What was he like the last time you saw him – on that Saturday? Come on, Justin. Was he talking funny or unusual or … Did he say he was gonna do anything?"

"No. I suppose he was a bit quieter than usual. But we just hung out. Then he went home – I thought he was at yours all this time."

"Did he tell you he wasn't playing the game tonight?"

"He didn't. I haven't even spoken to him today either."

"You missed him in school?"

"He wasn't at school. He didn't turn up."

"Oh, Lord."

Justin just stayed mute on the other end. I hated

him. The coward.

"Right, Justin. I need you to give me the number of that Carly girl."

"Carly's number?"

"Yes, do you have it?"

"I do yes … but why do you want it?"

"To see if she's seen him recently. Give it to me, please."

"Two seconds."

He fumbled about on his phone and then read out the digits. I jotted them down.

"Thanks for your help, Justin."

"No worries. Mr Ballard – do you think Caspar might have hurt himself?"

"Why would you say that? Did he mention something like that to you?"

"No not really. I'm just fretting now. I honestly thought he was just there at yours the whole time."

"If you find out anything just give me a call."

I hung up. Useless kid. No courage. If my best mate was under threat I would be animated.

Carly's number was there. I pressed the digit line and then gave it a call. It rang for quite some time and I thought it would go null, but then this mousey voice popped up.

"Hello?"

"Hello there, I'm sorry to bother you. It's Ralph Ballard here. I got your number off Justin. He gave it to me."

"…"

"So, I'm Caspar's uncle."

"Yeah."

"I met you one time at the house."

"Yeah."

"I wouldn't have called but, I think Caspar might be missing. And I'm panicking. Trying to decipher where he could be."

"Ah."

"Justin said that you and him broke up recently. When was that?"

"That was Tuesday last week."

"Has he called you since then?"

"A few times."

"When last?"

"Thursday, I think."

"Did he suggest that he might do something to himself?"

"What do you mean?"

"As in, harm himself?"

"No."

"All right. There's something else I need to ask. And just tell me straight. I get that you and Caspar were lovers. So you must've fooled around a lot and gotten to know each other's bodies, right? So you must've seen his chest at one point. Naked chest. That correct?"

I felt like a psycho, saying all of this. And her silence at the far end confirmed this fear. But I continued.

"Just tell me. Did you notice any scars on Caspar's body? On his chest. That's all I want to know."

"Yes."

"You saw some scars?"

"Yes I did."

"Did you ask him about it?"

"I did. And he said he'd done it with a razor. You know, like a shaving razor. Some of them were barely scars: like he'd done them the night before."

"So he did it more than once?"

"I think so yeah."

"Why did he do it? Did he say why?"

"He was messed up about the car crash …" Carly was crying now, and she stopped and started, and I felt appalling for having upset her, "when his parents got killed. And he kept talking about how he couldn't forget that memory. Of the crash. He replayed it in his mind over and over and he could not get it out of his head."

"Okay. Carly: do you know where he might have gone? Justin said he wasn't at school today. Do you reckon he might be at his other mates or something? Is there somewhere he went on walks?"

"Umm. I don't know."

"Anything you can think of?"

"Well. Sometimes he would go off at night. To the woods behind my bit. You know where the church is? Redburn Church?"

"I know it yeah."

"He stayed over at mind a lot. Which was nice. But there were a few times when I would wake up and he wasn't there in the house. He would sneak out. At night. And then come back later and I'd ask him where he was. He'd say he was walking in the woods behind the church. It was a bit weird. But if there's anywhere I can think of then that might be it."

"I appreciate your time, Carly."

"Ta. I never meant to hurt Caspar."

"Nor did I."

"I feel guilty that he's gone missing."

"I do as well. But, I will find him. I know I will."

36

I drove down to Redburn Church.

The church was tired and forgotten and the retiring sunlight on its falls was medicinal against its shut walls and windows and atheism.

I found an alleyway, in which to park, a short distance from the church. And walked down to the woods.

There was a path which led there, I knew of, and I hadn't been here in a long while. This pathway which cut away from the church and the housing and it turned woody. And as I walked down it the sides of it had been visited recently by a council team.

They had shredded up the nettles and weeds, ivy, and cut the branches from the trees above the path. Just mashed it all up with their machines.

And underneath it they'd severed the grass as well.

The blades of the grass lay across the stones of the path. Damp dead fecund flags. And I smelled their rich smell and it went into my nose, my head. That profound racy gaudy smell of cut grass.

Only humans would destroy grass. And then revel in the sentience of it.

What exactly was I expecting in the woods? To spot him straight out? The Redburn Woods were pretty big for a city woodland.

And so now I was wandering about these mazy paths, wondering what relevant skills I had in being here. And, once again, the woodland was immensely beautiful but it couldn't ease my panic. Just made me more lost than I already was.

At length on one of the trails there came a middle

aged woman walking her dog. This overweight cocker spaniel, which came fluffing up to me and swishing its tail.

"Excuse me?" I hailed the woman and she looked up at me nervously. "I don't suppose you've seen a boy around recently?"

"A boy?"

"Yeah, like a teenage lad. In the woods I mean. He has dark hair ... is quite handsome. Seen anyone like that along the paths today? He's my nephew."

"Umm. No I don't think so."

She edged towards the other side of the path and continued walking past me and dipped her head and called her animal to come with her. Onwards I went. I went through a band of birch trees with their silver boughs and gold leaves. Until I heard this weird medley of human noises ahead and I thought I was going batshit crazy and only imagining them ... and then I remembered that there was a lil kids' playpark in this lower section of the woods.

With swings and slides and I came out of the trail and beheld it. There were tots playing in there and mothers yacking on the benches at the side. I went up to the mothers. (In the park they had one of those rope climbing frame things in the big dome ((are they called spider frames?)) and there were children perched up there and I envied them, being small and not having to deal with things like familial terror just yet.)

"Hi there ladies," I said to two of the women who sat on one of the benches. They studied me and didn't say anything. "Have you seen a teenage lad around recently? He's sixteen; my nephew: I'm looking for him."

"Hmm ... I don't believe so. Why?"

"I just would like to find him. He's got brown hair and is quite nice looking."

"We only got here ten minutes ago with the kids. And didn't see anybody else on the trail, sorry. Are you all right? You look like you're freaking out? Is your nephew okay?"

"I do not know if he is – that's what I'm trying to find out."

"Oh. Is he ill?"

"I think he might have ... Urgh. It's okay."

"Can we help in any way?"

"If you see a lad of that type then please tell him that his uncle's looking for him."

"We will."

I dove away from them.

There were other people in the park too who I could have queried but I felt like I'd terrorised those two women already and couldn't stand the sounds of the children so I took a new trail north and the noises behind me died away and then I was searching through the trunks of the trees for movements of people or anything in twitchy mania.

I walked up down and across those myriad paths for hours. When I remember it now it does have a dream-like edge, a nightmarish labyrinthian zeal to it.

I'd see something in the wilderness – a shape or a colour – and I'd think it had something to do with Caspar. At one point I saw something red, between a cluster of ferns, and I went off trail and inspected it. It was a jumper. Dropped and left in the woods and my crazed mind went *that's Caspar's jumper! His body must be nearby!* But it wasn't even his size and he didn't wear any red jumpers.

There was this other part where I smelled woodsmoke. (Which is a scent I've always adored.) And I followed it and found this band of people who were around Caspar's age. When I saw them around a fire in the distance I thought *ah, he's just camping with his mates here. It's all good.* And I emerged out of the growth, on them, and one of the teens went, "I think somebody's coming."

There was a heavy funk of marijuana.

Four of them in total and when I got closer they stared edgily and I beheld that they were maybe early twenties rather than Caspar's age.

I asked them if they'd seen this boy with these descriptive qualities. They were baffled. I think they thought I was going to attack them or something. And they weren't responding. So I left into the forest again.

And then it started to rain. Insidiously light at first, these specks of liquid which were pleasant on the skin.

With the clouds came darkness. Dimness, rather, and I looked at the time and had no clue I'd been wandering about for three hours already. The rain surged. I got literally lost in the woods as the water thrashed everything in sight. This berserk anthem of foliage crashing. And I was soaked within minutes. Reduced to being just a stupid man in the forest.

I cursed and gurgled until I discovered a map. If I headed south from here I would find Redburn Church again. So I did that. And the journey back was me versus the elements. It was actually quite a rush to be battered by a summer rainstorm, quite thrilling to be razed by it. It pummelled me. It won.

And eventually I got back to the path which led to the church. The one from earlier with the chain-sawed shrubbery and mown grass. No smells. In this deluge – the rain gave no hope of scent because it slashed up the oxygen. My shoes trudged through the slushy vegetation.

The church was alit, now that it was night, in a friendly orange.

I found my way back to my car in the alleyway the backside of the church.

I got inside and spent five minutes sitting in the driver seat, breathing, and bemused at how much of an idiot I was. I took my coat off and turfed it in the back seat. The rain hammered the roof.

Then I looked down at my shoes.

They were choked with cut grass. Smothered with a mâché of wet green ... and now that I was out of the rain, its pong infected me.

I took my shoes off. And opened the door. And scooped up the grass off the shoes and flung it outside onto the road. This was tricky. The muck got all over my hands. I didn't want the grass strands on my pedals or in the car at all or anywhere. And the rain was making its tantrum noise again outside. So I finally got pissed off and I thought *fuck these shoes* and I just tossed them outside onto the cement. And shut the door again.

And drove home in sock feet. *I have other pairs of shoes at home. It doesn't matter.* The drive back was pretty smooth and was enjoyable wearing only socks.

Whence back in my driveway I got out and went up to the house and of course the socks got sodden instantly and I went through the front door and peeled them off and went barefoot into the kitchen and put them in the washing machine and then took the rest of my clothes off too and stuck them the same place and then I was completely naked in the kitchen but I hadn't turned the lights on yet. I went upstairs in the darkness. And showered. New clothes. Charged my phone. To check whether Caspar had called.

Nothing.

There was my bed. I lay on it. Exhaustion flumed over me.

I felt guilty to want to sleep because it was my duty to keep up the search for him. But you must know when you have fresh cotton on you and are warm and dry and are lain down after such a relentless day ... your body goes into standby.

37

My phone woke me up.

It was 3 a.m.

It wrangled beside my head on the other pillow. And immediately I was annoyed with it. Then my brain snapped a different way and I shot up and sat and picked it up.

NO CALLER ID said the screen. I pressed answer.

"Hello?" I begged.

There was this bleep bleep bleeping sound in the background, was the first thing I noticed.

"Hi there, Ralph?"

"Yes? Caspar?"

"Yes, it's me."

"Caspar, my friend."

"I'm in hospital."

"You're *what*?"

"I slashed my wrists."

I gasped. He didn't go on. So I went on instead.

"Caspar. We need you around to do important stuff. You can't do that to yourself."

"Listen, uncle. The nurses are needing to stitch me up. Don't worry about the background noises. The machines. They're just pinging because my heart rate is fast."

"So your wrists haven't been stitched yet?"

"No."

"Well is it life threatening? Are you still bleeding, Caspar?"

"I don't think its life threatening, no. I did a poor job. As always. I can't even figure out a way to kill myself properly."

"Which hospital are you at, Caspar?"

"I'm at –"

And just then the connection quit and I was cut off from him.

38

I instantly tried calling back but because it was from a hospital I couldn't get through to them – it just went to this silent blip.

I panicked immensely for about 200 seconds because I thought my nephew was going to die and that this would be my fault. Then adrenaline kicked in. And told me to get out of bed and figure out which hospital he was in.

We lived on the south side and there was a massive hospital not too far from us. An A&E and I figured this was the best shot. So I got in the car and drove down.

I sped the whole way. This was at three in the morning, remember, so there was no traffic. I deliciously rammed past a red light. Nothing mattered to me more than seeing my nephew alive.

Will he die? He said he wasn't stitched up yet. Will he bleed to death before I get there? Please don't let him perish. This isn't happening. This won't happen.

Then I was in the hospital car park. There weren't many vehicles en masse and I drove up as close as I could to the building and parked. Then rushed through the automatic doors.

The reception area was blindingly citrus. A man was working at a computer at the desk and I went up to him.

"Hi there, sir. I'm looking for a Caspar Ballard. I believe he's in this hospital. I'm his uncle."

"Okay. Tell me the name again?"

"Caspar Ballard," and then I told him his date of birth and then he began to type on his keyboard and then I said, "he called me just under half an hour ago and said he slashed his wrists. Please tell me where he is."

He flinched when I said the words and he kept squinting at his screen.

I took out my driving license. And showed him it, because I knew that hospital folks won't let you see a patient unless they know you're a relative.

"I'm his uncle. His legal guardian."

"Okay. Yes. Your nephew is here. He's in Block C. Which, you'll get to easy if you follow the pink line."

He pointed towards the pink line. It led down this spanning corridor unto the helm of the building.

"Thank you sir."

And I embarked.

The pink line was fat and healthy and I clung to it with relish. I went through endless doors and hallways with different lighting … and in my panged mental state the shapes everywhere changed, lengthening and shortening in this kaleidoscope mind. I got into Block B. There was a cleaner lady mopping the floor and this sting of chemicals hit my nose. She got a fright when she saw me. And then I had to walk over the floor that she'd just mopped and I said sorry and she glared at me and I left marks all over her hallway and I walked on.

The pink line turned left at the end of this corridor, towards a pair of thick doors. I went through them and was in an icily aired stairwell. Then the line disappeared and there was a panel on the wall which said BLOCK C with a diagonal arrow upwards. I walked up the stairs. These amazing echoes from my heavy breathing spun around the walls and the stairwell was stark and fearsome and could have been anywhere on the planet and eventually I got to the top where the stairs ended and there was a new set of doors with C on it and I entered.

I pursued another arrow which said RECEPTION and then I was at a desk with a young woman there. I told her I was after Caspar and he was my relative.

"Please tell me he's still alive," I said. A globule of my sweat dripped off my chin and landed on her desk and she pretended not to notice it.

"Let me just see what it says here," she said, looking at her computer. "He is in Ward 3. If you head there."

I was already off jogging. There was Ward 1. Where I passed people sleeping on open beds and there was a nurse who shooshed me for being too loud when I went through. Ward 2: wherein there were closed doors and I didn't see a single person.

Then I was in Ward 3 and there was a man who was walking towards me who was obviously a doctor. He was tall and bald.

"Doctor, sir," I said, "I'm Caspar Ballard's uncle. He cut his wrists. And they said he's in this ward. Is that correct."

"Yes, he is."

"He is alive?"

"He is alive, yes. His injuries were not fatal. I saw him when he came in: he didn't sever any of his main arteries. Are you his father?"

"I'm his guardian. His father's dead. I'm his uncle."

"Okay. Well, the nurses are still working on him. There's no need to panic, sir, your nephew will live. We'll need to give him a tetanus shot before he goes and we might have to let him stay the night."

"I need to see him."

"Sure, but the nurses are working on his wounds right now. They won't be that much longer though.

Will you wait on one of the seats for us? And we'll let you know when you can go into his room."

"I will, yeah. Cheers, Doc."

He led me to this small plastic chair in one of the empty offices. Which must've been a storage room, filled with drawers and medicinal tubes and tubs etc.

All the mistakes in my life had led me to this situation and I was paying for it now and I felt like a horrible bastard, just felt like one of the worst individuals alive. Belonged in Hell. I knew that Caspar would survive. And wondered how worse it would be if he'd bled to death on the drive here. I don't know what I would've done if so.

(Remember when I told you about that time I got my head kicked in by those three goons when I was in my thirties? How I reckoned it was my 'lowest moment'? I was wrong when I wrote that. This moment in the hospital, waiting in this storage room, was the worst point in my existence.)

Time can't measure such periods of pain mathematically.

But eventually the doctor from earlier came in and said,

"You can come and see your boy now."

And he led me to a room. The door was open. I peered inside.

Caspar was sitting upright on his bed. Calmly. He was naked at the torso and still had his jeans on and there were these long bandages tied down both his arms.

"I'll leave you two to it," the Doc said.

"Thanks Doc."

I went inside. And the door closed softly behind me and then Caspar was looking at me. His eyelashes were huge and slick and glorious. Across in the corner of the room they/he had taken his shirt off. It was a beige shirt and it was totally stained with blood now, as if it had been dipped in a vat of dye, this lush dark red colour. I wondered whether the stains would ever come out. Caspar's coat was there too, intact. He still had his shoes on – they were hanging off the end of the bed.

"I'm so sorry, uncle," he said. My lil nephew.

I gulped and I didn't want to respond to him verbally because I didn't want to cry in front of him so all I did was up and offer him a handshake and he accepted it and I felt his cold palm and tried with full honesty to warm it with my body heat.

39

Lots of folks have mentioned the goal I scored against United. The volley. Aye, it was a sublime moment.

But it's not my favourite goal of mine.

You remember the opening bit of this book? When I lived next to the park as a kid and I'd head out there in the infant mornings to practice with myself? Well, I went down there a lot in the social times, too, and played about with the other lads. I had no friends, for obvious reasons; but I enjoyed the charge and gusto of competition between males – it made me feel worthy. I joined other games whenever I could. A lot of the time I got rejected: a group of boys didn't want me to play with them. But I persevered. And it gradually turned the other way; many of the groups wanted me in their team because they needed my skills.

It confused a lot of them because I was young and smaller and yet better than most of them. (All of them. Ha.)

And there was this one time when these older lads came down. By 'older' I mean that they were maybe fourteen or so and I was half that age and so they seemed like giants to me.

They were from the upper district from our one. From a different block of the city, I mean, and most of us were scared of them. I wasn't. And elected to join the game. They laughed, and let me in. And I got playing. And they realised pretty quick that I was good.

So they chopped me whenever they could. Dirty fouls. Raging slide tackles. It wasn't just me; they did it against the whole of our side. The local lads. And our team completely cowered out. Apart from me. I was that young that I still believed I could be a proper player one day.

Was still a boy. One pure version of Ralph Ballard. Regardless of alcohol or autism or any other form of malfunction. I was far less afraid at that age.

They tripped me, shoved, swiped, poked, studded me.

I kept playing.

They were already winning by some margin. I think it was 8 – 0 to them or something absurd as that.

And I led the kick off after they scored their eighth or whatnot goal.

But before I did, I spoke to the forwards who were in our team. These were Rob and Sean. And I said to them,

"We've got to get a goal in, friends. Sean – if you take a run down the wing. Rob – if you bolt towards the box, I shall pass it up to you. If you hesitate a little a bit and then pass to Sean on the wing. Sean can then cross it in to me and I'll definitely be there. Okay?"

They nodded. The goons behind us were all laughing and enjoying their colosseum gore.

I kicked the game off. Rob passed it back to me and then bolted up field. I dummied one of the opponent strikers who sailed at me, and then passed the ball up to Rob. It could have failed. But was instead perfect. Rob trapped the ball. He waited, like I'd told him to. Then I thundered towards the box. Whilst Sean tanned down the wing.

One of the goons rammed at Rob with a tackle. And Rob dodged it and waited for Sean to get to the wing. Then swung the ball out to him. Sean collected it with his left foot. And there were no goon defenders near him. I was in the box. And I hollered to him,

"Sean, I'm here for you. I'm here for you Sean." and he passed to me. This long bird-swooning-like pass which I can still feel the fathom of. Sportsmen know that desire for the ball, something that's theirs, that's adamant and proud for their ownership.

I caught the ball. There *were* goons around me now, in the box. Two of them lunged at me. They both slid in to me at the same time, so I chipped the ball over both their bodies, and these flakes of mud flew up under their oafish frames ... and then I was one on one with the goalie and I just whacked the ball beyond him into the corner of the net.

Sean and Rob came running towards me and they jumped into me and I hugged them back.

40

So we must be at the epilogue now, right?

I'm sixty something now. And live on my own.

Caspar's at university these days. He's studying. Enhancing his mind.

There's nothing further dramatic I need to tell you about me.

Only that, I had a dream the other day.

Wherein I woke up, within the dream. And my father was calling to me in his abrupt disciplinary voice:

"Come and help me in the shed, son," he yelled.

So I got out of my room and went outside into the garden and the wood pigeons were cawing lusciously. With their hypnotic 'coo coo – coo coo' chant. The grass was thick and heady and I was decades back in time when insects were still prolific and I wiped the flies off of my face and went into the open door of the shed.

Where I saw my father inside. And it turned stuffy immediately; the scent of sawdust and oil and, of course, Dad's pipe-smoke aftermath.

"Something I wanted to talk to you about, son," he said.

"Okay? What's the job?"

"It's not a job. I have to show you something."

He took out a box from his complex desirable shelves. It was sealed up with brown tape. I recognised it immediately.

"Did you seal up this box, Ralph?"

"I did."

"Why?"

I didn't answer. And then he pulled out a Stanley knife and gestured to cut the tape off and I protested.

"So what's in the box?" he said.

"…"

Dad knifed the tape off and pulled the cardboard covers up and he beheld what was inside.

Smashed glass.

"Smashed glass," he said. "Why did you do that?"

"I didn't mean it."

"Why did you hide it?"

"I thought you would get mad if I put the shards in the bin."

"Your mother says you smashed the milk bottles in the garden."

"No. I just dropped them by accident. And I didn't want to make you angry and that's all it was."

And then my father thundered towards me with his volcanic eyebrows. He was going to beat me. I ran out of the shed.

THE END
Harrison Abbott
4th – 21st June 2022.